Books by William Campbell Gault

The Sunday Cycles
Two-Wheeled Thunder
Through the Line
Dirt Track Summer
Drag Strip
Dim Thunder
Rough Road to Glory
Bruce Benedict, Halfback
Speedway Challenge
Mr. Quarterback
Gallant Colt
Mr. Fullback
Thunder Road

THE SUNDAY CYCLES

WILLIAM CAMPBELL GAULT

DODD, MEAD & COMPANY   NEW YORK

Copyright © 1979 by William Campbell Gault
All rights reserved
No part of this book may be reproduced in any form
without permission in writing from the publisher
Printed in the United States of America

1 2 3 4 5 6 7 8 9 10

Library of Congress Cataloging in Publication Data

Gault, William Campbell.
The Sunday cycles.

SUMMARY: Two 18-year-old cousins graduate from a little "Sunday fun" to dirt tracks, desert racing, and motocross.
[1. Motorcycle racing—Fiction]   I. Title.
PZ7.G233Stp   [Fic]   79-52049
ISBN 0-396-07715-3

For Bill Cox . . .
an even older pro

1

We're only forty-first cousins, or something like that, but Aram always acts as if he's my father—or at least a Dutch uncle. He *is* five inches taller than I am, and fifty pounds heavier. But he's a month younger. And if he's smarter, I never noticed it.

I guess almost everybody in Cameron is related, if you go back far enough. If you went back a couple of generations with a third of the people in town, you would be in Armenia. That's where my father's parents came from—to escape the murdering Turks. Today, Armenians don't come to America. You can't escape the Russians.

Aram is all Armenian, and so are his names, Aram Sarkis Bedrosian. I'm only half; my mother is Scotch. She thought Colin would be a nice name for her first born. So that's my name, Colin Sergenian. Most people call me Sarge.

We are partners in a service station, Aram and I.

We leased it the day we graduated from high school from the man we had worked for since we were sophomores.

I handle the drive and the lube rack, Aram the engine work. Except for cycle engines; we both work on those. We have this wrecked dirt bike a customer left behind for an unpaid bill.

We rebuilt it, with the idea of selling it. But halfway between Cameron and Fresno, there is a rough, banked third-of-a-mile dirt track where all the good ol' country boys gather every Sunday to play gasoline cowboy. The Sunday after we finished rebuilding the bike I talked Aram into trucking it the fifteen miles to this dusty madhouse to join the fun.

The three-lap opener was action enough for him. It was too short a track and too small a bike for a 190-pound six-footer.

For a man of efficient size, both the track and the bike fit better. There were no officials to tell us where we finished in any of the sprints. All we kept track of was the winner. I finished in the same lap as the winner every time.

On the way home, I said, "We could round up some officials who understand track racing and some volunteer handymen to fix up those fences. We could get that thing organized."

"We? Who's included in the we?"

"All true lovers of engine sports," I said.

"You mean motorcycles."

"Or midget cars or go-karts."

"Midgets cost money, and karts don't run on that kind of surface. Motorcycles, you mean. Don't include me in the we."

"Okay, killjoy. You can be my mech."

"And who'll watch the store?"

"Who watched it today? Who watches it every Sunday? Lee. When did we ever work on Sunday?"

Nothing from him.

"I asked you a question, Aram."

"I know. You're right. We hardly ever work on Sunday."

About two miles of silence, and I said, "What's bugging you?"

"It wouldn't be only Sundays," he said. "You know that. I went the route with you, didn't I? First Soap Box Derby and then go-karts and then drags. You at the wheel and me with the wrench. I thought that was all behind us."

I laughed.

"What's so funny?" he asked.

"Nothing, I guess. Well, I mean—you make it sound as if we're ready for the rest home, at eighteen."

"Who's talking rest home? Crazy guys taking crazy chances on a beat-up cycle track, running machines without brakes? Just because a man doesn't

11

want any part of that scene, it certainly doesn't mean he's ready for the rest home."

"That's true," I said.

"We've got a solid business, Sarge. In a couple years we should have enough salted to make a down payment on the property. Is that rest-home thinking?"

"It certainly isn't. You always make sense, Aram. You are a natural merchant, true to your heritage."

"Aw, shut up, *odar!*" he said.

That's as close as I can come to the American spelling, *odar,* meaning *other,* meaning non-Armenian.

When we pulled up behind the station to unload the bike, Lee came out to help us. He looked between us and asked, "What is it this time? What are you two fighting about now?"

Lee is Aram's brother, a soph in high school. Levon is his Armenian name.

"I don't want to talk about it," Aram said.

Lee looked at me. I said, "I want to have a little Sunday fun out at that deserted track but big daddy disapproves."

"Sunday, huh!" Aram said. "Sunday for starters and then Fresno on Friday nights and Bakersfield on Saturdays and—"

Lee smiled at me. "Was it fun?"

"I thought so. It would be more fun if it was

organized. I guess Aram didn't like it. You know how clumsy he is with machines."

"Enough, enough, *enough!*" Aram said. "Let's drop the subject."

"We can do better than that," Lee said. "We can sell the bike. That kid from Clovis was here this afternoon. He offered three hundred."

"Considering," Aram said, "there aren't more than four parts from the same manufacturer on the entire machine, that's a good offer. I'll take it."

"I won't," I said.

Aram looked at me too coolly. "You want to give me a hundred and fifty for my half?"

I said too hotly, "I will. You want to buy my half of the business?"

He stared at me in surprise. I glared at him. Lee said, "Cut it out, you two! Grow up!"

Aram continued to stare at me. "What brought this on?"

"*Odar,*" I said, "for one thing. Since when am I an outsider?"

He smiled his paternal smile. "I apologize. Now admit I am more than a merchant. I am one of the finest haywire mechanics in the San Joaquin Valley, am I not?"

I nodded.

"Partner," he said, "you can have that dumb cycle. I donate you my half of it."

13

I shook my head. "I'll pay."

"No," he decided. "We'll own it together. I'll go with you to that dust bowl every Sunday to see that you don't break your fool neck."

"Yes, papa," I said.

My real papa was watering the gray crabgrass of our front lawn as I pulled into the driveway. I had washed my face and hands at the station, but my clothes were still heavy with dust.

"Racing again," he guessed. "Somewhere, on something."

"At that deserted track on Highway 41, on a motorcycle. Who owns that property?"

"A man named Muldowney, a Fresno land developer. You'd better change your clothes before your mother sees you."

"Why? I come home dirty every night."

"Not track dirty. Your mother has this innocent notion that your racing days are finally behind you."

"It's just for Sundays," I said. "Just for fun."

He smiled. "Of course. Why did you want to know who owns the property?"

"I was thinking, if we patched the gaps in the fence and rented a grader and a roller to smooth out that track, we could run some organized races."

"I see. Just for Sundays, just for fun?"

"Of course," I said.

My mother claims I am too competitive because

I am Armenian. My father argues it is because I am Scotch. Aram has this dumb theory that it is a major flaw in all small people.

I am five feet, seven inches tall and weigh almost 140 pounds. I do not consider that small, and I do not consider myself too competitive.

My sister Berjouhi considers it is restricted to males. She is two years younger than I am. She would graduate from Cameron High School in June, valedictorian, president of the senior class, head cheerleader, county debating champion, student voted most likely to succeed. The pot thinks only the kettles are black.

Monday and Tuesday were busy days at the station. I had to wait until Wednesday afternoon to go into Fresno and talk with Melvin Muldowney, known as "Big Mel" throughout the Valley to his friends—and enemies.

He had a small office at the end of a long corridor in a two-story building on Shaw Avenue. MELVIN T. MULDOWNEY, the lettering on the door read. OIL OPERATOR. ENTER.

I entered. He was big, and so was the hat on his head, a white cowboy hat, and so was his smile. He was sitting behind a small desk. "Well?" he said.

"What's an oil operator?" I asked. "I thought you were in land development."

"I am now. I used to be in oil. I didn't change the

lettering. What's on your mind, son?"

"That track you own," I said, "between here and Cameron."

"Oh, yes. What's your name?"

"Colin Sergenian. I was wondering if you'd let us fix up the track at our expense and run some real races there."

"Who is *us?*"

"All the guys who have been racing motorcycles there on Sunday afternoons. Didn't you know about it?"

He shook his head. "I usually go to Reno on weekends. What do you mean by *real* races?"

"I mean organized. I mean with a *paid* starter."

"Who'd pay him?"

"The riders could all chip in."

He tilted that big cowboy hat onto the back of his head and looked at me thoughtfully. "What kind of show is that, where the actors pay?"

I didn't have an answer. I guess he wasn't expecting any. He was looking past me, at some kind of dream shaping up. Big Mel, dreamer. "It wouldn't be hard," he said, "to stretch out that track. There's a wide streak of adobe at that north end. Just a matter of grading it. We could throw up some stands along that west straightaway easy enough."

He took a deep breath and smiled at me. "You know, Colin, I've been in the wholesale produce business and the oil business and in real estate. But I've always had this hankering to be in show business."

I said, "I don't think any of the boys out there are professional riders. Most of them are from Valley ranches."

He nodded. "That's where our fans will come from, too, our customers. And those ranch boys are handy with tools. I can charge the lumber, but my cash flow isn't what it should be this month." He took another big breath and gave me another big smile. "I'll bet you could organize all the volunteer labor we'll need."

Operator was the right word, I realized now. "I can try," I said.

Some of the workers I rounded up were station customers, some of them men I'd met at drags and at kart races. They weren't dumb; they knew Melvin T. Muldowney was using them to his own advantage. But (we told ourselves) we were going to have a nice Sunday playground.

One of our amateur riders owned an equipment rental business. He had a grader heavy enough to extend the north end of the track. We wound up with half a mile of banked hard clay, which is not easy to find in the San Joaquin Valley. And every foot of it was fenced.

Two-by-eight fencing on six-inch posts can be put

up by rough carpenters. We could qualify as that. But then Mr. Muldowney decided he wanted a refreshment stand, and he wanted the kind that would require the work of finish carpenters. He brought some in.

"Your cash flow must have improved," I said.

He stared at me doubtfully for a few seconds. Then he grinned. "Who got cheated? Look at the track you boys have now."

"For how long?"

He frowned. "I'm not following you, son."

"We don't have enough fans to support a refreshment stand. Only the big names can bring in crowds. You must be planning to run professional races."

He nodded. "I've arranged to lease some temporary stands." He put a hand on my shoulder. "The big names don't scare you, I'll bet."

"Big names don't scare me, but big men do, Mr. Muldowney. Some of my biggest and meanest customers worked on this track. I sure wouldn't want them to think I conned them."

"They'll have no reason to," he promised. "Every meet I run will be an open meet. Every event will be open to both amateurs and pros."

We were standing near the almost finished refreshment stand. It was late on a Friday afternoon and the highway was busy with traffic both ways.

18

The campers and trailers were heading for the ocean, the ranch families were heading for dinner and a movie in Fresno.

"A lot of money is spent on recreation in this country," he said. "And a lot of money is being made on it."

"Especially for a man who has learned to cut expenses," I said.

He sighed. "Sarge, think of me as sharp, if you must. But don't think of me as chintzy."

2

If my doubts about Melvin T. Muldowney seem too cynical for a boy of eighteen, consider that I had been working at one job or another since I was ten, and had been a partner in an adult business since I was sixteen.

I had known the slow payers and the no-payers, the cheaters, the liars, the overextended, the opportunists.

As of now, Mr. Muldowney had been guilty only of that last. When Colin (Opportunity) Sergenian appeared at his door, he had been ready. It had been *my* idea to improve his track with volunteer labor. Not one of us slaves had been in chains; we could have quit at any time.

He had said he was not chintzy. He wasn't. He hired veteran starter Doc Kucera from Bakersfield for our opening program. He lined up some experienced scorers. But he didn't do what I hoped he might do, attract some of the top-line pros.

The professionals who did show were all local boys. The big names were probably afraid that they'd lose their AMA cards if they competed at an unsanctioned meet.

"What we have," Aram said, as we were unloading, "is a longer track and the same familiar faces."

"The bikes look newer."

"Same bikes. They washed 'em."

I nodded toward the next pit. "How about that one?"

It was a shiny new Honda, equipped with Fox shocks. "Nice," Aram said. "It's Brad Gehrig's. He has finally got the edge on you, Sarge."

Brad was the youngest, and the best, of the local pros. I had competed against him often, but never on a cycle. I had been riding a cycle, off and on, since I was fourteen, but not in competition.

"Show is not go," I said.

"Let's hope you're right. This mongrel of ours would certainly not win a show ribbon. Where's that number your sister made for us?"

Most of the amateurs had crudely painted numbers on pie tins wired to the front of their machines. Berjouhi had enameled a scarlet "66" on an octagonal piece of sheet aluminum and covered it with a clear lacquer.

"A touch of class," Aram said, as he clamped it

below the control cables. "We'll go down with a touch of class."

"Down? Why down?"

"Look around you. What do you see? You see all the good ol' boys—and about half a dozen pros. You see the backyard-tuned bikes and the pro-tuned bikes."

"Don't be modest, Aram. Nobody in the county tunes a cycle any better than you do."

"But what did we have to work with?"

We had 125 cubic centimeters of Aram-modified Delta Oriole two-stroke. The company was no longer in business. We had some homemade parts and some scavenged parts; everything but new parts. In the saddle of this patchwork special, we had a rider with very little competitive experience.

So what? Wasn't I here only for the fun?

Brad Gehrig was in his pit now, along with his mechanic brother, Joe. "Well!" he said. "Finally!"

"Finally what?"

"I finally get my revenge. Does that thing run?"

"Only on Sundays. It's good to see you, Brad."

"I'll bet. It guarantees you won't finish last."

I shook my head. "I don't expect to beat any real dirt bikes, not with this."

He smiled. "Sarge, save that for strangers. You always expect to win."

Hope, Brad, not expect. We all hope to win, or we

wouldn't show up. It wouldn't happen today, but once I got some experience on dirt. . . .

There would be three five-lap sprints that would act as qualifiers for each feature. There would be two thirty-lap feature races. There were, I think, actually more riders than spectators this opening day of the new and newly named Muldowney Raceway.

Brad and I didn't tangle early. He was in the first sprint, I in the third. There was only one pro among the ranch hands in Brad's field. He took a first. There were three pros in my field, and they all finished ahead of me, as did some others. I finished sixth. If I had finished below that, I would have been out of the feature.

Three bikes had tangled and gone down in the last lap of that sprint. If they hadn't, I wouldn't have qualified. They had all been ahead of me. I had tried to learn, watching the pros in front take their lines in and out of the turns. All I had learned was how to eat dust.

Aram was grinning when I came in.

"Ha-ha!" I said. "You enjoy seeing me look foolish, don't you?"

"Don't make it personal. You weren't the only clown in that race. Are we here for fun, or for blood?"

He had me there. I said nothing.

"You qualified," he said.

I nodded.

"It's Brad's turn to beat you, for a change."

"Brad's and a dozen others. We should have sold this machine to that kid from Clovis."

"He's still interested," Aram said. He paused, to study me. "You don't plan to give up this nonsense. Why would we sell the bike?"

I didn't answer.

He nodded. "I get the picture. We'll mortgage the business and buy us a bike worthy of you, and—"

"Don't be silly," I said.

"I won't if you won't. Sarge, this machine can stay with ninety percent of the cycles here. Once you learn how to handle the track, there'll be no reason for you to be embarrassed."

"You're right," I admitted. "Forget it. Just an idea I had."

"And still have," he said. "Let's move. They're starting to line up for the feature."

There would be eighteen bikes in the first feature race, some 250's but mostly 125's. If I could keep my steed upright, I would probably finish in the top half of the field. Half of the entries in the sprints had not finished. In a thirty-lap race, the toll should be even higher.

What a way to think—if I could stay upright, I might finish ninth! What kind of target was that, to finish ninth? What was I doing, starting to think like a loser? Everybody loses more often than he wins, but who plans a career of losing?

"Stop mumbling," Aram said, "and get your helmet on. They're waiting for you."

Eighteen firing cycles, most of them two-strokes, can shake the earth and rattle the brain. Eighteen digging wheels would soon stir up enough dust to blot out the sun. I was going into this organized disaster area underequipped and inexperienced— and looking forward to it. If you can understand that, start saving now for your first bike.

I was in the second row at the jump-off and well short of the first turn, when the Suzuki directly in front of me swung high for an early line into the slope. I had a doorway to the front runners.

A twist of the wrist and I went digging up the ridge to front the Suzuki. This was the route the sprint winners had favored. Rolling down the bank into the backstretch, both of us were moving faster than the bikes below. We were nose to nose halfway through the stretch, and leading the field.

At the end of the lap, I was second by less than a length. I was going as fast as my present skills would permit, and so was the ranch hand on the Suzuki. It seemed logical to expect the better men on faster bikes would soon be challenging us.

They didn't. What was even stranger, we didn't

lap *a single bike* that was still running; the only bikes we passed were down. In thirty competitive laps we had maintained positions as fixed as the wooden horses on a merry-go-round.

There were some boos from the stands, but there were more laughs, as we droned through our insurance lap. In our pit, Aram was smiling. In the next pit, Brad's big brother was scowling.

"Something fishy is going on," I said. "What?"

"Don't complain. You finished second."

"What happened, Aram?"

"Oh, the good ol' boys were having a little fun out there."

"You mean they were blocking the track behind? They were boxing out the money riders?"

He nodded, grinning. "Something like that."

"That's not funny, Aram."

"Relax, Sarge! What is this, the Dirt Track Nationals?"

From the next pit, Brad said, "We can make it anything you want, Aram, including war. But this is too good a track to be turned over to hoodlums."

"Watch your language, punk!" Aram said.

Then Joe got into the act, being closer to Aram's size. "Who are you calling a punk, purple foot?"

"Cool it," I said, "both of you. Brad's right. We could make this place another Ascot. This is a race track, not a playpen."

"This place," Aram said, "will be exactly what Mr. Muldowney wants it to be. He's here for the money and he must know that feuds are great attendance builders."

"Well, they're not for me," Brad said, "and I'm going to tell him so."

"I'll go with you," I said.

Melvin T. was sitting at one of the tables behind the refreshment stand, consuming a double cheeseburger. He looked at us doubtfully. "You have the look of men bringing trouble."

"Did you watch the feature?" I asked him.

"Of course. Great show. Every motorcycle that was still running finished in the same lap. That kind of show will bring them in."

"Mr. Muldowney," I said, "it was supposed to be a contest, not a show."

"You finished second, Sarge. Why are you complaining?"

"I don't want to run that way. It was phoney. Didn't you notice?"

He smiled. "There were some shenanigans going on between the country boys and the slickers, but I sure didn't arrange that."

"Didn't Doc Kucera complain about it?"

"Not yet," he said, looking past me. "But I think he's about to."

Doc Kucera was coming up from behind and

breathing fire. "I won't stand for any more of what we just had, Muldowney. If you intend to run this kind of track, I'll go home right now."

Mr. Muldowney said mildly, "There's nothing wrong with this track that I noticed. If there's something wrong with the racing, that's your problem. You're in total charge of that, Doc."

"Total?"

Muldowney nodded.

"Okay!" Doc said. "Sarge, you and Brad spread the word to your people, no boxing, no blocking—or they get flagged off the track. That was the first hippodrome finish I've seen in fifty years, and it's the last one I want to see."

As we headed back toward the pits, Brad said, "I really admire you, Sarge."

"No kidding? What's the stinger?"

"You just finished second the only way you could possibly finish that high, and still you—"

"And I don't want to hear the rest," I said. "Brad, once I get the hang of this—"

"Of course," he said. "You've *always* been a winner. Let's spread the word to our people, as the good doctor suggested."

Nobody is *always* a winner, as we all know. Today was going to be an also-ran day after that phoney second place. I had too much to learn.

I didn't have to qualify in the second series of

sprints; my finish in the first feature had qualified me. My *crooked* finish had qualified me in the first row of the second feature.

As there had been in the first, there were eighteen cycles in the second thirty-lapper. Six bikes didn't finish. Which meant that any bike that kept running couldn't finish worse than twelfth.

I rode the bike that kept running that finished twelfth. Playing it safe, concentrating on staying upright, I finished twelfth—three full laps behind the leader.

"There has to be a reason," Aram said. "The bike's not that slow and you're not that gutless."

"So, if I pushed it, I might have finished seventh or eighth and only *two* laps behind the winner. What's so hot about that?"

"It's better than twelfth."

"Not enough to risk a spill. I want to learn this track, the hard spots and the soft spots, the right lines in and out of the bends. To do that, I have to stay up and running."

Aram sighed. "That's what you call Sunday fun?"

It was. To become good at something, to learn how to do *anything* right, is bound to make it more fun. The abiding joy of excellence is what my mother calls it.

Once I learned what I intended to learn, this bike would not be fast enough. That could mean another hassle with Aram. I had enough money to buy a different bike, but I didn't have enough money to pay a mechanic as good as he was. Without Aram's wrench, I wouldn't have had any need for my trophy case at home.

There was no point in looking forward to an argument that might never happen. There was always the worse possibility that this three-hundred-dollar orphan would prove to be as much machine as my skills deserved.

We did better, both of us, the next week. The Oriole didn't load up as much under deceleration; she answered the throttle quicker. I took a fourth in the first sprint, behind three pros, one of them Brad Gehrig.

At the refreshment stand, he told me, "You're getting too good. Aren't any of your gang going to join the AMA?"

"I doubt it. Why should they? This isn't their profession."

"I know. Well, it's none of my business—"

"Speak your mind," I said. "You always have."

"I'd like to see this track get an AMA sanction. This is one great plant you guys put together here."

"Thank you. Muldowney isn't going to apply for an AMA license unless it means more money in his pocket."

"It could. If the Association finds out some of us

members are racing here, they'll make us quit. I'm sure Muldowney can't keep this operation going by selling hot dogs to ranchers' relatives."

"True enough," I admitted.

"Somebody ought to explain it to him," Brad said.

I knew whom he meant by "somebody" but I pretended not to. I said evenly, "I think you're right. One of your older AMA members should explain the whole setup to him."

I was not an unreserved admirer of the American Motorcyclist Association, under that or its original name. I had joined it when I bought my first bike. It had been the American Motorcycle Association then, and its non-racing members, I thought, got very little in return for their membership dues.

Many of the racing members must have felt the same way; some of the sport's biggest names were constantly in dispute with AMA officials. *But*—it was national. It was staffed with totally honest if not totally capable officials. *And*—competitive motorcycling has always been oversupplied with wild men on high-powered and precarious two-wheeled machines. *So*—somebody or some body has to lay down the law. You stick with what you have until you can do better. What we had was the AMA, an established body of well-intentioned men.

Finishing fourth in the sprint, and first among the amateurs, had me convinced that my careful and disciplined approach to my dirt track self-education was finally paying off.

The early going in the feature strengthened that feeling. The first ten laps were pure chaos, rank amateur hour at Muldowney Speedway. Bikes went tilting into the fences, sliding down the banks. Defensive driving was the answer; simply surviving should put a rider up with the leaders at the finish.

I steered clear of the wild ones and tried to keep Brad's Honda in sight, following his line when I could see him through the heavy dust, remembering his lines when I couldn't. I challenged nobody. Attrition would do the advancing for me in this one.

In the fifteenth lap, Aram's waving slate informed me I was riding fifth. That had to mean we were less than a quarter of a lap from the leader, because all four bikes were still in view as we streamed into the south turn.

In the sprints, a downed bike was out of the running. In a thirty-lap run, there was time to regain lost ground. I was riding in the same lap with the leaders; the bikes behind weren't.

Attrition could no longer do it for me. If I wanted to hold my place, I would need to fight off the challenges from behind. They began to come up in the twentieth lap. It was back to one-on-one.

The four bikes ahead had pros in the saddle. Most of the riders who came up to challenge were not. Let me modestly relate that I fought them off, each in his turn. Let me humbly record that the speed of our duels was not fast enough to carry me into contention with the pros in front. Though I fought off every challenge, I still finished fifth.

"You're getting the hang of it," Aram said.

I nodded.

"You seem to be the best of the amateurs," he said. "The pros, now—"

"Have better bikes," I said, "as you explained to me last week."

"And more skill," he said. "This bike's good enough for you now."

Now? Aram had said *now!* Was he starting to think my way? I didn't ask him. It was too early. He hates to be crowded. I said, "Fifth place qualifies us for the second feature. Let's watch the sprints from the other side of the track. I'll buy you a hamburger."

We watched two of the sprints from there. Then Aram went back to check the bike and I went over to sit next to Melvin T. Muldowney, who was at one of the long redwood tables, counting his money.

"It's good to see you," he said. "I had no idea when you walked into my office that historic Wednesday afternoon that a whole new world would be opened to me."

"Money can't be a new world to you, Mr. Muldowney."

He stared at me sadly. "It's depressing to see cynicism in young people."

"I was joking, sir. I know you're enjoying the racing. I came over to alert you."

"Trouble—?"

"Not yet. But I think some of the professional drivers here are worried about their cards. They'll probably demand you get an AMA sanction."

"Thanks for the warning, Sarge."

I shook my head. "It's no warning. I think they might be doing you a favor. You may not know it, but you've got a fine track here. It's too good to be a farmers' playground. The AMA sanction could upgrade it."

He nodded. "Thanks again." He smiled. "You know, I have this feeling you don't totally approve of me, but you're on my side."

I shrugged.

"Some day," he said, "I hope I can prove to you what a real friend I can be."

3

All of our traveling local pros were what are called "privateers" in cycle racing. That meant they paid their own way. Eventually, the economics of the trail would force most of them into other lines of work. The few who became good, very good, the few who became champions, usually wound up as factory riders. These were the teams that manufacturers supported for promotional purposes.

The Muldowney Raceway got its AMA blessing in early May. It got its first factory-rider entries the Sunday following.

"Good-bye, good ol' boys," Aram said. "The real pros have come to town, now that they can win Pacific Division points here."

"It had to happen," I said, "once it was sanctioned."

"Tell that to the boys who bent their backs for no pay."

"They'll still be here. They're all joining the AMA. The ones who want to run as amateurs will be scored separately in the mixed fields."

"Who worked that out?"

"Doc Kucera, Melvin T., Brad Gehrig, and your humble partner."

Four pits north of us, Army Elkins, last year's National Number Two, was working on one of the several bikes he'd brought. Aram looked at him, at me, and then down at our battered steed. He frowned.

Say it, Aram, I thought. *Say we need a new horse, or horses. Say it!*

"Are we running with the pros?" he asked.

I nodded.

"Will there be any big bike races?"

"The finale. It will be a mixed field. Just an experiment."

"Sunday fun," he said. He glanced toward Elkins' pit, back again at our orphan, and shook his head. "Have fun, kid."

Winning is not the only fun in competition, not if you love your game. But not having a chance to win can bring the fun down to its minimum.

Mr. Muldowney had a winning hand now, offering the public three different groups of heroes, the local stars, the national stars, and the good ol' boys, each group attracting its own fan club. He raised the price of hot dogs a nickel and hamburgers a dime.

The extra income from these sources, he explained, would be used to increase the purses of the contestants. The extra income from increased attendance would be used to increase the purse of Melvin Muldowney.

"Don't look so gloomy," Aram said. "Fixing up this track was your idea, remember."

I nodded.

"That new carburetor should give you more zap. And, Sarge, you've never really crowded this machine."

"I know."

"Why not crowd it today, especially on the jump-off?"

"I planned to," I said. "Aram, don't you have more fun here than you do at work?"

"Well—yes—sure—"

"So, if I buy a new bike, you'll still come out here with me?"

He looked at me levelly, and I knew the word was coming, the word from old Uncle Aram. "Learn to walk before you run," he said. "Learn to handle this machine and I'll go halves with you on a better one."

He was hooked. Grumpy was hooked. It wasn't *all*

business with him. It couldn't be. When you tune a bike as well as he does, you want to see your labor pay off.

I was in the first sprint, and the field looked mean to me. A pair of strangers in expensive leathers on slick Yamahas were in the row ahead. They weren't street bikes, and the men didn't look like rookies.

But they were strangers to the track. They hit the first turn too shallow, well below the groove. There was room above them that led to room in front of them. That is where I wound up.

Getting out in front early is a big advantage in short sprints. Your vision through most of the race is free of dust, there is no need to work out passing strategy, and the risk of collision is small. To top it all, your ego is fortified.

The new carb responded well to demands, feeding the rich juice needed. The Delta Oriole went whining through the backstretch, showing them all her heels, feeding them all her dust.

The Yamahas trailed by inches, one high, the other low, like twin vultures, waiting for a sign of faltering. But the little Oriole, the last of a vanished but not vanquished breed, had too much stubborn pride for that. She sang on, neither coughing nor spitting, riding the groove like a train on a track, giving yours truly his first-ever win in a motorcycle race.

"Beautiful!" Aram said. "Do you realize who you beat?"

"Fourteen other riders?"

"I mean those two who were pressing you, those two on the Yamahas?"

I shrugged.

"The Dunphy twins," he informed me.

Dan and Don Dunphy were Yamaha factory riders. Both of them had finished in the top twenty nationally every year for the past three.

"The track was new to them," I pointed out.

"Not completely. They were practicing on it when we got here this morning. This little Oriole may be enough machine after all."

I didn't argue with him. The way I saw it, the afternoon would prove him wrong. He was already half-sold on a new bike; it was the wrong time to argue.

We had built a better mousetrap here. They would all be heading our way, the top boys on the beautifully tuned works machines. Even Aram wasn't enough of a magician to get the Oriole ready for that kind of company.

That was a good afternoon in one way, bad in another. It was good for my confidence, bad for convincing Aram we needed a faster horse. The second feature would be open to everything up to 500 cc's. The first was limited to 250's and below. All but three of the riders entered were running 125's.

There were five team riders on factory bikes in the first, including Mr. Number Two, Army Elkins.

He had the fastest time in the qualifying sprints, and it had won him the pole. I, too, would be on the pole—in the second row. Mine must have been a slow field. I was starting in the seventh slot.

On the Muldowney Raceway, where the best footing on the front stretch is the lower track, the seventh slot is a fine launching pad, despite the six in front. It is even better when the rider in front of you believes in getting out early and running away.

At the flag, Elkins' Husqvarna took off as though it had been catapulted, leaving a clear lane open for lucky me. There was no way this Delta was going to catch him. But, as I saw it, one bike's dust was bound to be lighter than the dust from six bikes. I put the spurs to the Oriole.

There were other cycles on the track that could top out higher than Elkins' Husky. There was none that could dig out of the bends quicker or accelerate better through the middle range.

His line was different from the one I favored. I knew the track better than he did; he knew his business better than I did. We finished the first lap one-two, the Oriole only two lengths behind and running easily.

There would be no hippodrome finish today to

guarantee me second place. And though I try to avoid negative thinking, it didn't seem likely I could finish this high against the men and machines in this field.

Three laps later, it looked more hopeful. Aram's slate informed me the third-place bike was a quarter of a lap behind. One of the reasons came into view as we slid out of the south turn. Four bikes were down in the backstretch, two of them works machines. Both of those riders were new to the track.

Ahead of me, Elkins was changing his line, searching for the groove. Ahead of him, a tailender was just entering the north turn. With only four laps gone, it appeared I was already closing in on the laggards. The Oriole showed no signs of strain, barely edging into the red zone.

The tailender pulled into the pits, coughing and smoking. There were no other cycles in sight, and Aram's slate told me the third-place cycle was narrowing the gap. We weren't catching up on the field; they were catching up to us.

Elkins got the same message. His Husky whined higher, glancing pebbles off my number plate, his rear wheel fantailing a geyser of blinding dust as he spun up the bank, trying for a new route into the turn.

I stayed below the dust in my personal groove. I lost no ground through the turn and gained none.

Playing second fiddle to Army Elkins was good enough for the moment. When the challenges came up from behind, I could always revise my strategy.

Four laps spun by with no change and no challenge. If there had been any threat from behind, Aram's slate would have informed me. A lap later, there were two letters on the slate—"OK."

Okay so far, riding an easy second to National Number Two on a track I knew better than he did. I had helped to grade it, to fill in the few soft spots in that rock-hard adobe. Okay so far, but only an innocent infant would expect this blissful state to continue. I was an old man of eighteen.

With the Dunphy brothers in that pursuing pack, with most of the hungry privateers still running, the action would have to get hotter. Somebody should be making his move soon.

It didn't come soon; it came late. In the twenty-sixth lap, Brad Gehrig's Honda and Dan Dunphy's Yamaha escaped from the tangled traffic behind and moved up to make their bids.

Elkins saw them before I did, and took off. Dunphy went after him, as Brad and I fought it out high on the bumpy rim of the north turn. Those Fox Shox gave him better traction there; he cut down the bank at the peak and led me into the front stretch.

Dunphy and Elkins were well ahead of us, closing

in on a three-cycle clot short of the pits. Both of them were moving too fast for the traffic. One of the laggards moved wide to pass—just as Dan and Army, hub to hub, tried to get past him.

It took some miracle riding to avoid disaster, which they did. Both bikes swerved wildly toward the stands, glanced off each other, regained traction, and gunned back toward the groove.

But Brad and I were there now, moving at full speed. Dunphy, on the inside, pulled higher to give us clearance. Again, their cycles made contact. This time they both went down.

The trio ahead had strung out; we lapped them all before we hit the end of the backstretch. Two local boys were now riding one-two in a star-studded field.

The local boys rode one-two all the way to the checkered flag. It would be nice to report that I was the one before the two, but Brad led every foot of the way through the final four laps.

"Great!" Aram said. "Plenty of bike and plenty of rider."

"And second-place money and second-place points," I added. "Brad's Honda did better. And there are faster bikes here than that Honda."

"It wasn't his engine that beat you," Aram said. "It was his suspension. We can correct that."

I was too weary to argue. "We can try," I said.

43

My finish had qualified me for the second feature, the mixed-field windup. The scoring would be separate for each class, the field fuller and probably faster. There would be only a half-dozen 500's; I had a feeling the boys riding them would be entered strictly for the practice. Mr. Muldowney had announced during the week that future meets would limit the windup to 250's and above.

He had enough actors now; he could put on any kind of show he wanted. He had already talked to several riders about building a motocross course in the infield.

Aram and I were metering out the oil for our fuel when Army Elkins came over from his pit and introduced himself—a modest touch.

"Brad Gehrig tells me you guys built this track yourselves."

"Not quite," I said. "It was a third-of-a-mile track, and we extended it."

"You did a beautiful job."

"Thank you."

"Brad also told me you haven't been riding long."

"Not in competition."

"Well, whatever, you're very good at it. You hung in there for a long time."

"Until you decided to run away."

He smiled and shook his head. "I didn't. The

Husky did. Luck." He winked and went back to his pit.

"A real gentleman," Aram said. "Even if he doesn't know much about engines."

"Nobody's perfect," I said. "Let's get a hamburger."

My stubborn friend should get a better test of our mount in the final feature. My second-place finish today had not been dishonest, but it had been freaky. Too few bikes had stayed vertical. Once these tigers here on the hot cycles learned to read this track. . . .

Under the eucalyptus trees behind the refreshment stand, Brad and his brother sat at one of the tables, munching hot dogs. We joined them.

Brad was still wearing his victory smile. He said, "Back to the wars, right, Sarge?"

"Whatever that means."

"You know what I mean. If you'd had a better bike under you, I'd have finished second."

I shrugged.

"I knew you wouldn't spend the rest of your life pumping gas."

"That part's true," I admitted. "The way our business is growing, we'll be hiring more help in a year or two and I can stay in the office."

Brad laughed.

Joe said, "Don't mind him, Sarge. He's nervous. He isn't used to winning."

Aram said, "We could show him our books. I'll bet you not many of those so-called stars out there earned as much as we did last year. You can't eat trophies."

"Right!" Joe said. "That's why I'm going to night school."

Brad said nothing, smiling his knowing smile, basking in his victory.

We had earned ourselves a front-row start in the finale, Brad on the pole, I flanking him. There were a number of better men on faster machines behind us. Brad was no longer smiling.

"Luck," I said.

"Thanks. You, too. We'll need it."

He anticipated the flag better than I did, having the pacemaker's advantage. He had more torque than I had, the inside route, and more experience. These are known as alibis. He built a ten-foot gap between us before we hit the turn.

Two larger machines had passed us high, but that was a separate war. Brad and I had started our personal competition at the age of nine on homemade karts powered by chain-saw or lawn-mower engines. In the karts, and later, in the drag racing, I'd held a narrow edge.

That had been a four-wheeled world. This was a

world of precarious balance and traction, a world of different skills.

We passed some bikes, some bikes passed us. In a mixed field, a rider needs help from his pit to know where he is. Brad was still within range in the eighth lap when Aram flashed a big chalked "4" on the board.

Among our peers, we were riding third and fourth. I had a feeling Brad was not going all out. It was too early to challenge. With more than twenty crowded laps in front of us, we both could pick up ground without a challenge.

Some cycles went down, but not the two in front of us. We still rode third and fourth halfway through the race. In this field, this late, on this machine, I shouldn't be in fourth place.

Two laps later, Dan Dunphy came up on his snarling Yamaha to confirm my opinion. He had passed me, and was crowding Brad, before I had a chance to react.

Brad must have seen him earlier; his Honda had upped its pace before Dunphy had cleared me. They charged the north turn under full steam, sliding high on the bank and gunning down into the front stretch with advantage to neither. I inhaled their dust and rode clear of their action. Unless they could defy the law of gravity, simply staying vertical seemed to be my best bet for third place.

While I hung back, waiting for the inevitable to happen, Dan's twin on his matching Yamaha sneaked past me below, heading for the duel in front.

If I wanted to be a spectator, I could sit in the stands. There was still some reserve in the Oriole; we moved closer to join the fun.

Dan and Brad were leading, Don above them and two lengths behind. There was solid footing below him in the south turn. I used it to make my bid.

The inevitable I had been waiting for happened. Brad's bike hit a soft spot and went skidding sideways down the bank just as I got there.

I tried to get outside, swinging sharply up the bank toward the fence. But my front wheel caught his rear wheel broadside and we went bouncing toward the timber.

Luckily, I missed the post. But not the two-by-eight. The Oriole stopped there. I went over the handlebars and over the fence and into a waiting bramble bush.

4

My leathers were deeply scratched by thorns, my helmet dented. I was dizzy and my right ankle throbbed, but I was whole. I stood on the lower rail of the fence where I could be seen in the pits, and waved to let them know there was no need for an ambulance.

Below me, against the inner fence, Brad's Honda was on its side. Brad was standing in the infield, looking down on it, probably wondering if it was too late to get back into the action.

There was no way I could. The front wheel on the Oriole was egg-shaped. I sat on the grass behind the fence and watched the parade go by below. Neither bike was in a traveled lane; the yellow flag didn't wave.

Aram brought the pickup around when the race was over and he could get out of the infield. "You okay?" he asked me.

"I guess. I think I sprained my ankle. Who won our class?"

"The Dunphys—in a dead heat. They were so far in front they held hands and coasted across the line together." He crouched over the Oriole. "It's only the wheel. The fork's not bent. We've got a lot of wheels."

I should have bent the fork, I thought.

"You were doing all right until you got ambitious," he said.

"I was riding sixth at the time."

"That's pretty good. If you'd have hung back, you would have had clearance enough to miss Brad."

And then I would have been fifth—pretty good to Aram, not to me. I said, "I don't think it's sound winning strategy to assume every other bike in the race is going to tip over."

"That isn't what I meant, Sarge."

"I know. Let's go. My ankle's swelling."

We loaded the bike and climbed into the cab. "A first and a second," he said. "Why are you sour?"

"I'm not sour!"

He swung the truck down the grassy bank to the service road and headed for the highway. There, while he waited for traffic to clear, he said, "Okay, we'll buy a new bike."

"Not yet," I said. "I'm not sour, Aram. I'm still shaken up by the fall."

"Well, when you're ready, we'll buy a new bike."

A first and a second. . . . I had lied; I had been sour. Probably because Aram had told me what I knew, but refused to admit.

If I hadn't challenged Brad when he rode alone, why make my move when he was battling two other riders? It wasn't the first time my impatience had hurt me on a track. There had been plenty of laps left.

At the station, Lee said, "That kid from Clovis was here again." Then he saw the bike. *"Eeek!* There goes three hundred bucks!"

"It's only a wheel," I said. "And the bike's not for sale, not yet."

"That little three-hundred-dollar orphan," Aram told his brother, "earned us eighty-five dollars today."

Eighty-five dollars is not bad pay for a Sunday afternoon. If we were racing for a living, eighty-five dollars would be skimpy pay for two men for a week's labor.

Aram was right; we probably earned more at the station than ninety percent of the riders on the trail. But even Aram would admit they had more fun.

At home, my father asked me, "Why are you limping?"

"I took a little spill." I paused. "And a first and a second."

"Congratulations. Try not to limp where your mother can see it."

By now, of course, Mom knew I was racing motorcycles. But so long as Aram was with me, she didn't complain. Aram is her idea of the truly solid citizen. She suspects he must have at least one Scotch ancestor.

We put a new wheel on the Oriole that week and beefed up the suspension. We experimented with a new spark plug that was supposed to resist carbonization and overheating, thus eliminating pre-ignition.

It did all of these things in the advertisement but not in the Oriole. We went back to the old brand.

The way Aram labored over that bike, it was easy to believe he, too, was hooked on racing. It was probably something I believed only because I wanted to. He worked just as religiously on customers' cars.

Melvin the showman came up with a new card that Sunday. He decided that one five-lap opener and four twelve-lap races would be better for attendance.

This would give each of his three audiences a chance to see their favorite win. Starting positions would be determined by lot.

The five-lapper would be all amateur. The next three races would be open to both amateurs and professionals, but restricted as to engine classes. The finale would be a sixteen-bike showdown, open to the top four from each of the previous races. He had doubled the purse for that one.

We went to the track early on Sunday to get in some practice and test the new suspension. It was better. It was fine.

When I pulled in, after five fast laps, Aram said something which turned out to be prophetic, in a strange way. He said, "That is one little sweetheart. There is no reason she should be an orphan. There aren't any manufacturers today putting out a sounder machine."

"It's not completely a Delta any more," I pointed out.

"The engine is," he said. "Let's get a hamburger."

"First tell me why you wanted to sell it for three hundred dollars if it's such a classic."

"It's a racing bike," he said. "At the time, I didn't think we would ever have any need for a racing bike."

We went across the track and had a hamburger. We got to talking with the gang under the eucalyptus trees until it was time for the first race to start.

It was too late to get back across the track. So we had another hamburger and watched the five-lapper from there, the country boys in the opening free-for-all.

The races to follow were bound to look dull after that one—except to those fans who admired skill.

They charged the banks and bounced off the berms. They scraped the fences, rarely kept the front wheel on the ground, and went down in droves. The four in front who qualified for the windup were not exactly winners. It would be more accurate to call them survivors.

It was easy to see why there was a longer lapse between the first and second races than there was between the others. The track had to be regraded.

"Was that what we called Sunday fun?" Aram asked me.

"It still is—to them."

"I see. Now, we're experts?"

"Not yet. Patience, partner."

Probationary novice is the way I was classified in the AMA. I would be competing against my superiors in the 125 cc twelve-miler. In any sport, your best chance for improvement is to compete with your superiors. And there is always the possibility, you must remember, that they are not superior.

The luck of the draw put the major threats in the last row. The Dunphy brothers, Brad, Army Elkins, all of them would have to fight through traffic if they hoped to advance. That should make the competition more interesting.

Big Mel had drawn the numbers from his big hat. It would be unfair (and much too cynical for a youth of my age) to suspect the great man had been guilty of shenanigans.

The pole had been awarded to an amateur from Fresno. I was on the other end of the same row. Between us, in the front line, were a number of young riders on old cycles.

My experience on the lengthened track had been limited to five-lap sprints and thirty-lap endurance tests. My strategy would remain the same. Try to break out in front early and enjoy the clean air as long as possible.

It almost worked. The only dust I absorbed was the amateur's by the time we hit the first bend. I stole a technique from the country boys, climbing the bank to the berm, bouncing off it at the peak, and accelerating downtrack into the back lane. Two straight lines are often shorter, and quicker, than a curved one.

I hit the backstretch groove with enough clearance and led all the way to the north turn. He beat me there, finding an inside route better than mine, taking the first lap lead.

He was running a new Yamaha and he was running it well. He could take a first without costing me a nickel, but I wasn't here for the money in it. The pros behind us who raced for a living were. We should be seeing them soon.

The first of the breed I saw was my semi-friend, Brad Gehrig. He had been in the last row with the Dunphys and Elkins. They were probably still biding their time. We were only in the third lap, less than a quarter of the way to the flag. Impatience had cost me a wheel last week; I let Brad go by.

The Fresno amateur took it more personally. His Yamaha quickened its pace as he and Brad fought it out for the lead through the grandstand turn. They were nose to nose and twenty yards in front of me as we swept past the pits.

Aram's message board was waving. It showed two letters, a hyphen, and an exclamation point—"E-Z!"

Easy is right, Aram, with nine laps to go. There is no need to remind me. We could run out of wheels.

Not loafing and not pressing, I kept the pair ahead in range into the turn and into the backstretch. They were moving faster than I was through the straightaway.

Only one of them was moving faster as I hit the grandstand lane again. The Yamaha was on its side against the fence at the peak of the turn. Brad Gehrig and Colin Sergenian were again riding one-two with only eight laps to go.

Behind us, the last-row tigers were starting their moves. Army Elkins was a quarter-lap behind, the Dunphy brothers only a few yards behind him. Crowding them was Gary Park on a Harley, Number Fifteen, nationally.

I carefully, not impatiently, twisted a few more revs out of the Oriole and began to creep up on Brad. He was running a current Honda and I an orphaned Oriole. But Aram was right—again. There weren't any manufacturers today building better machines than the defunct Delta company had.

Brad took the low road into the south turn. I stayed with the country boys' strategy, bouncing off the berm. Brad was downshifting, trying to dig out of a slide, when I went by him and into first place.

I had a short reign, the king for only a lap and a half. Gary Park whined by in the backstretch of the fifth lap. Elkins cut below me and gunned past in the north turn of the same lap. Behind, both Dunphys were closing in.

This patience can be overdone. When Dan Dunphy got closer, I took off.

He had more low-speed torque for the heavy, rutted turns, but the Oriole had a big edge on those hard straights. I picked up more there than I lost on the turns. With a lap to go, the pair ahead were again in sight, riding in close tandem into the south turn as I moved past the pits.

I gained on them steadily through the turn, into the backstretch, and around the last bend. There was a straight, hard track in front of me now, and they were, I thought, still within reach. Though I was high in the red zone, and winging, I bottomed her.

I heard the clang and then the bang before the back wheel locked. For the second time in a week, I was heading for the upper fence. I missed it by inches and came to a stop still upright, but out of the race.

The piston had blown, the way I figured it. I had blown a piston, and the rod had jammed in the cylinder wall. Had impatience cost me another high finish? I didn't think so. The track had been clear when I made my move.

Aram would think so, probably. Aram didn't believe in *holding* an engine open, only in spurts. He would give me one of his Dutch uncle lectures.

I was wrong. "Metal fatigue," he explained in the pit. "It happens. She's been to the wars too often. It has to be the piston, don't you think?"

I nodded. "The rear wheel locked. The connecting rod has probably ruined the cylinder wall."

"Right." He sighed. "We have a dead horse, Sarge."

Nothing from me.

"I'll miss her," he said.

"So will I. Let's load her up and go home. I've had enough for today."

Who can mourn a dead machine? Steel and rubber, leather and plastic, without soul, what is there to mourn? The human ingenuity that designed it, the careful workmanship that built it, you can mourn the untimely end of that. And a machine that never quit until it died? It had been a better machine than I had been a rider.

"Don't sulk," Aram said, on the way home. "We'll find another."

"The good ones cost a lot of money."

"So, we'll find one that's almost good and make it better."

Monday was a busy day at the station, and so was Tuesday. Wednesday afternoon was slow enough for Lee and another student to handle. Aram and I went into Fresno to see if we could find a horse that we could afford.

The ones worth buying, we couldn't afford. The ones we could afford weren't worth buying. We dickered for the worthwhile ones without success and left an offer behind, in case they changed their minds.

"We could check the ads in the cycle magazines," Aram said. "Or maybe Brad would know where we could find one. He's got a lot of friends in the business."

Brad had friends with cycles: flat track and motocross, trail and street machines. All but the street machines were battle-worn and tired. The street machines were too bulky and too expensive.

"Back to Fresno," Aram said. "We can stretch the budget."

"No hurry," I said.

He stared at me. "You're really down, aren't you? What is it?"

"I'm not down. It's just that anxious buyers rarely get any bargains. Let those dealers we talked with in Fresno simmer a while."

"Sound merchant thinking," he agreed. "I've been a good influence on you."

We got a call from Fresno on Saturday afternoon, but it wasn't from a dealer. It was from Melvin T. Muldowney. "I'll be seeing you tomorrow, won't I?"

"I planned to work," I said, "and give Lee a Sunday off. I guess you know I don't have a cycle."

"I wasn't sure. There are some people from San Jose I want you to meet. They're the people who bought the Delta plant and patents. I was talking with them this morning, and your name came up."

"Why would my name come up?"

"Because I brought it up. They've built a couple of prototypes and plan to go into production soon. They're looking for a young tiger who isn't signed up, and who can get them some publicity."

"If they want a factory rider," I said, "they can do a lot better than Colin Sergenian."

A silence. And then, "You make me sick. You really make me sick. When you're not cynical, you're negative."

"I'm sorry. I apologize. Thank you, Mr. Muldowney. But I can't go traveling around the country. We're building a business here."

"Be at the track tomorrow," he said, and hung up.

"What was that all about?" Aram asked. "What did you mean about traveling around the country?"

"Some people have bought the Delta plant. Isn't that in San Jose?"

He nodded. "And they want you?"

"Mr. Muldowney suggested me to them. Don't ask me why."

"Because he owes you, that's why. What makes you think you'll have to travel around the country? There are plenty of pros who never race east of the Rockies."

"Not factory pros."

"Sarge, don't jump the gun. You listen to what they have to say. I'll watch the store for Lee tomorrow."

5

We all got together at the Muldowney table under the eucalyptus trees, the table nearest the snack bar. The moneyman was Curtis Loft, tall and thin and elegant, from San Francisco. The factory man was Lars Dykstra, also tall, but neither thin nor elegant, more of a country boy. But he was a graduate of Cal Tech and had been chief engineer of the original Delta company.

The way they explained it to me, they planned to make only 125's for at least the first year. Their plans for the future included nothing larger than 250 cubic centimeters.

"Small, quality motorcycles," Dykstra explained, "have always been a Delta tradition. When we shifted to those road hogs, I fought it, unsuccessfully. They might have been the reason we went bankrupt. Our machines are going to cost a little more than the competition's, because of our limited production. We think they'll be worth the extra money."

"I hate to sound modest," I said, "because I'm not. But there are some young local pros who are a lot more experienced than I am that you could sign up."

Loft smiled. "I notice you didn't say 'a lot *better.*' We've signed up one of them, Brad Gehrig. He's a friend of yours, isn't he?"

"More or less. We get along pretty well."

"I'm sure you will. We're on a tight budget and our support will have to be limited. But, if we're successful, both you and Brad will have exclusive dealer franchises in your home areas—if you want them. They might be worth money, someday."

"And how much traveling would there be?" I asked.

"West Coast only," he said. "We don't plan any eastern dealerships for some time. We hope to rebuild our reputation out here."

Mr. Muldowney said, "Aram would go along with that, wouldn't he, Sarge?"

I shrugged.

"He'd be a big plus."

"I know. I wish he had come along today."

"You could phone him."

I shook my head. "With Aram, I have to work slowly and face-to-face. I'm sure I can swing him."

Mr. Loft said, "There are other mechanics."

"Not for me," I said.

"You phone me," Mr. Muldowney said. "Tonight?"

"Tonight or tomorrow," I promised.

Aram had a customer on the drive when I got back to the station. I went inside and tried not to look devious.

"Well?" he said when he came in.

"I don't know. I told them you're not crazy about traveling."

"Me? What's it got to do with me?"

"Aram! We're partners!"

"Don't get cute, Sarge," he said. "Lay it all out, now, straight and clean."

I did that.

"And you thought you'd have to travel the country. Don't they have any factory mechanics?"

"I suppose," I said. "Muldowney agrees with me, though. You're our best bet."

He nodded, but he was thinking of something else. Finally, "That old feed store next door has been vacant for over a year. A Delta franchise might do pretty well in this area."

"Maybe. If they don't go bankrupt again."

He shook his head. "Stop it! You're trying to play me like a fiddle. I told you not to get cute."

"Okay, okay! Do we go?"

"We go," he said.

It would not be the Grand National Camel Pro Tour, nor the AMA Supercross or Motocross Series. But the same hot-shoes who built their national ranking in those would be here, too. I would finally have a bike to match theirs, and a chance to win some Pacific Division points.

Our first new Oriole was delivered on Tuesday. Mr. Dykstra brought it himself in a pickup truck. He and Aram went into the office for a two-hour briefing on the mechanics of the machine. I took over the Chev valve job Aram had been working on, and Lee came from home to handle the drive.

"They stayed with the same engine specs," Aram told me, when the briefing was over, "but they've improved the porting and the ignition. The suspension is better, too. We'll get a backup bike next week. Partner, I think we've got a winner!"

"Only if I am."

"Don't worry about it," he said. "Elkins and the Dunphys and Park won't be here Sunday. They'll be at that motocross in Los Angeles. You should do all right."

"Thanks for your qualified show of confidence. I finished the valve job. Why don't we run out to the track and get in some practice?"

"Why not?"

There were two bikes raising dust at the Muldowney Raceway when we got there, and a duplicate of ours in the pits. Brad and Joe were getting ready for Sunday, too.

"Here come our partners," Brad said. "Welcome to the big time."

"Teammates," I corrected him. "Does your bike have the new Lieder mag, too?"

Brad looked puzzled. Joe laughed, and said, "Be nice, Sarge. We're all in this together."

"Right!" I said. "Great machines, aren't they?"

Joe nodded. "I never could understand why they went bankrupt. They've always turned out great machines."

"And now they're better," Aram said. And added, "Partner."

"Partner," Joe agreed. "We'll keep 'em running and pray that these punks can keep 'em vertical."

In a competitive world, is it possible to be a true friend to somebody who is in the same trade—and doing better at it? It is possible, but it is difficult. I would have to work at it.

We took our trial runs at different times because we took them when Aram and Joe told us the bikes were ready. It could have been a coincidence that this happened at different times. Or it could have been their way to keep us vertical until Sunday.

Any new machine is going to feel more solid under you than an old one, but the feeling this machine gave me was far beyond that. The suspension was stiff without being jarring, the response in the lower speeds was quicker and topped out higher.

"It sure beats that Honda of mine," Brad said. *"Every* way. We should be able to compete with any 125 cycle on the market."

"It's a works machine," I reminded him. "We've never had a crack at a works machine before. But all the factory riders have them."

"They'll need 'em," he said.

I went to the track alone on Friday after work and got in almost two hours of practice before dark. Many of the performance characteristics of this machine were the same as the old. Where they were different, they were better. I didn't have that alien feeling of riding a strange new horse.

Summer was coming on fast, and summer is always hot in the San Joaquin Valley. We had picked the right time to tour the cooler sections of the state. Mr. Muldowney was preparing for July and August, building permanent covered stands to keep his customers out of the sun. Only the riders would roast.

He had wasted a lot of years in the wrong trades; he was a natural showman.

We small-town merchants probably have an automatic distrust of showmen. But he had, as he'd promised, proven what a real friend he could be. Colin Sergenian, greenie, was now a factory rider.

67

In the pits, Sunday, Brad said, "We should do all right today."

"That's what Aram thinks. You mean because the big boys are down at the Coliseum motocross?"

He nodded. Then, "Had any experience in motocross?"

I shook my head.

"And I've had very little," he said. "I wonder why they picked us?"

"Because we're comers, Brad."

I had no experience in motocross racing, and he had little. I had run in a lot of desert scrambles when I was sixteen, but strictly for fun. Mr. Dykstra had probably explained why we were chosen at last Sunday's meeting. Delta was on a tight budget.

According to an audience survey Mr. Muldowney had commissioned, the fan interest at the track was still strongly local. So last week's amateur opener was now a ten-lap affair, and the three twelve-lappers had been cut to ten laps.

We had gone from an opening-day card of eighty laps of racing to forty laps. That permitted more time between races to sprinkle and roll the track—and sell refreshments.

The early going in the opening cowboy free-for-all was tamer today. They must have decided that, over the longer route, patience can be an ally. The mood and the pace changed about halfway through the seventh lap. The clot of riders near the leaders began to grow.

As they came hammering around the final turn toward the checkered flag, they took on the bulk and the thunder of a cattle stampede, so closely bunched that at least a half-dozen of them had a good chance to win.

Three of them did, in a dead heat. An electric eye at the finish line might have distinguished between them. Doc Kucera's eyes weren't that good.

The crowd was still buzzing when the public address system informed them that the usual practice of dividing first, second, and third place money among the winners would not be followed. Each of the three would be paid a full winner's purse. In merchandise, of course. They were amateurs.

Sarge, think of me as sharp, if you must. But don't think of me as chintzy.

"I won't, M.T.," I said.

"You won't what?" Aram asked.

"I was talking to myself. Glad to be here, partner?"

"I guess. I'm not having as much fun as you are, though. Maybe I ought to ride in one of those openers. I'm still an amateur."

"Why don't you wait until Delta turns out some 250's? This Oriole is a light horse."

I had been joking, but Aram played it straight. "Good idea," he said.

Doc Kucera had drawn the numbers for starting positions today. Brad had won a first-row start, I a second. We were the only factory riders in the field, and our factory was not yet in production.

I had more experience now and a better machine. Why was I more nervous than usual? Probably because hoping was no longer enough; now I was *expected* to win.

Brad must have been harboring the same nervous thought. His Oriole jumped at the start as though stung by a hornet and hit the first turn far too fast for traction. He went sliding up the bank as most of his line and half of ours moved past below him.

I was, so far as I could guess, riding fifth or sixth. Brad, at the moment, had to be in a tangle with the tailenders. I expected to see him again before this race was over.

I was riding fifth, Aram informed me, as we finished the first lap. Twenty yards in front of me, a Suzuki and a Harley were fighting it out for fourth place. Beyond them, the leaders were still in sight.

Both of them took the turn too high. I didn't. Now they could fight it out for fifth place.

The third-place rider was the Fresno amateur who had given both Brad and me too much competition before he had gone down in my last race, two weeks ago, the man on the Yamaha.

I didn't know his name, but had a feeling it would

be well known some day. He was good. Meaning no disrespect to the honorable Yamaha, he could have been better than I was, but he was not astride an Oriole.

I tried to get past him low in the north turn, and bounce off the berm in the south. Neither strategy worked. He kept the gap between us constant for three frustrating laps, before I got an assist from the last place rider.

His cycle was smoking and sputtering along the inside rail in the backstretch. He was hoping to reach the pits without walking, as the Yamaha closed in.

For some reason, his bike veered right at that instant and the Fresno whiz kid swerved high to avoid him. There was room to go and I went, into third place.

The leaders were closer, less than fifty feet in front, as I rounded the near turn. Both riders were pros, both were running pure track bikes. It was a time for patience. There were still five laps to go. Soon, we would be running into heavier traffic, overtaking the laggards.

The traffic grew heavier, but it didn't slow the pair ahead. They threaded through it, less than a length apart, holding their lead over me.

Halfway through the ninth lap, their lead was the same. It was time for a little less patience.

I watched their early line into the turn. There should be clearance, I thought, if they didn't come diving down the bank too early. I gunned for the daylight.

The going was rough and heavy in the only route that was open, slowing me enough to make collision seem certain, as they headed downtrack.

I slowed. They must have, too. While we were scrambling to avoid each other, Brad Gehrig breezed past below, into first place.

We chased him, all three of us close enough to be burned by his exhaust. It was a great finish for the crowd, and a fine win for Delta, for Brad's Delta, not mine. I took fourth place.

"Thanks for the assist," he told me, in the pits. "That was sporting of you, tieing up those front-runners. That was team play!"

Nothing from me.

"I owe you," he said. "Come on, I'll buy you a hamburger."

"I prefer cheeseburgers," I said. "And I usually have two."

"Today, they're on me." He grinned, and put a hand on my shoulder. "So, I'm sorry. Sometimes I think I'm funny and I'm not. But Sarge, we're partners!"

"Okay," I said. "I'm a bad loser."

"You haven't had enough practice at it."

Lately, I have, I thought. I said, "I'll buy the Coke."

There was a lot of banter around the long table, most of it barbed. The losers took it with their grim smiles, the winners with their cheerful grins. I gave 'em my Mona Lisa special.

The two I had tangled with in the ninth lap were sitting across from us. One of them said, "You guys work well together. Who wins next time?"

Resentment bubbled in me, but Brad said quickly and easily, "We haven't decided."

I was glad I hadn't answered. Because the rider said, "Just a little joke, boys. I've watched both of you run in drags, and I know you both run to win. Delta made a smart move."

"We think so, too," Brad said. "Sarge should do better, once he gets the hang of it."

"It's time for my second cheeseburger," I told him.

Anything under 250cc's would be next. The only other factory rider in the field was Hans Nevel on a Marlowe. He had made the top forty last year; he had been thirty-ninth.

He had turned into a stormer this spring. There were rumors that he was about to lose his sponsorship, and would soon need to seek honest labor.

The luck of the draw gave him the pole. Brad and I weren't as lucky; we wound up in the last row.

Our luck changed about ten seconds after the start. Five of the front-liners charged the first turn, fighting for the lead. Only Nevel managed to stay vertical. Brad and I rode into the backstretch in sixth and seventh place, Brad in sixth.

I let him set the pace, and watched his line. Though I had helped build this track there were still a few things he could teach me about riding it. Our previous competitive history was only that—history. In this field, the edge was his. So far.

He didn't follow my berm-bounce technique. He rode the rim lower and got back to the straights just as fast. So, okay, maybe. . . . But when the traffic below was heavy, I planned to stay with the berm-bounce.

I had noticed, at the start, that he took the middle of the track, so he could move either way through the turn, to avoid the jam. Beginners have a habit of trying to crowd the inner rail, the shorter route. It is also the area where most bikes go down, in a beginners' scramble.

He carried that route through when moving up on jammed lappers. I followed him as we climbed from sixth and seventh to fifth and sixth, then to fourth and fifth. We were running out of laps by this time. With two laps to go, I made my move.

We must have been on the same wavelength. He took off when I did and kept his advantage. The leaders were in sight in the backstretch of the last lap. Either he thought they were still within reach or he was trying to increase his gap over me.

Whatever, he attacked that final turn at a pace even the Oriole couldn't handle. His bike went skittering up the bank as I sailed by below for my second consecutive fourth-place finish.

There were things I could learn from Brad—but a sense of pace wasn't one of them.

6

Hans Nevel, the stormer, had finished first on his Marlowe. There was some grumbling in the pits about his hell-for-leather tactics, but nobody entered an official complaint.

Despite his slide, Brad had finished fifth. "We should have won," he said. "In that field, we should have won."

"Both of us?"

"I meant either of us."

"Try once more."

"Okay," he said. "*I* should have won. And, if I hadn't been in it, you should have won. I sure set a dumb pace."

"Right," I agreed. "Next time I'll find my own."

Nothing from him.

"You staying to watch the windup?" I asked.

He nodded. "I want to see that Nevel on a big

bike, playing with the big boys. They'll straighten him out."

"You make it sound personal."

"We've had words a couple of times. The man's running scared. He's worried about losing his factory cushion."

Aram and I went home, to give Lee an extra hour of Sunday freedom. Those big bikes make too much noise and stink for me. And I would never, I hoped, be bloodthirsty enough to enjoy watching anybody get his comeuppance in a sport as dangerous as ours.

The story I got from customers on Monday—the windup had been a real donnybrook. A couple of Oxnard riders had tried to box him, some of the other big-bore boys had ridden him wide on the turns and generally harassed him. He had fought them all off and finished second by a nose.

He had continued his fight in the pits, putting one of the Oxnard riders to sleep with a haymaker. Only the timely arrival of a couple of sheriff's cars had prevented a gang war. Hans hadn't been the only Marlowe rider in the windup.

"Most of the customers I talked with," I told Aram, "seemed to enjoy that kind of show."

"I hope you didn't argue with 'em."

"You taught me long ago never to argue with a

customer. But with all those creepy gangs prowling the country on their hawgs, motorcycles don't need any more bad publicity."

"Sarge, none of the boys out at the track are Hell's Angels. You'll see more violence in a pro football game than any cycle race."

"I know. That's why I didn't go out for football in high school."

He shook his head sadly. "You didn't go out for football because there were no gasoline engines involved. And, of course, your size—"

There was a customer on the drive, so I didn't have time to answer. As a matter of fact, I didn't have an answer.

He was right. Even basketball was turning into a contact sport. And in baseball, when a runner is coming into second, there is usually dangerous action there if a double play is possible.

What burned me about the cycle gangs was the publicity the press loved to give them. They happened to be creeps who rode motorcycles. They would have been just as creepy without the machines.

But in the public mind, the vicious men and the innocent machines were linked as equally villainous. I guess it's called guilt by association.

We got our second bike on Tuesday. It wasn't really a backup track bike; it had been modified for the meet Delta wanted us to make on Sunday, a desert scramble.

It was the wrong time of the year to be riding in the desert, though the weatherman had promised us a protecting overcast. The meet would be held near Oasis City. This is in the high desert, and not to be compared with Death Valley. It was probably only a few degrees hotter than Fresno.

The big names would be there, along with a host of unknowns. The field was small, compared with most desert scrambles. There would be a hundred pros and amateurs riding a rocky, sandy, and hilly six-mile course for ten laps. Both Pacific and National points could be won there.

The suspension on the new bike had been beefed up, the gear ratios altered. I had a horse for the course, and I knew the course—unless they had changed it since I was sixteen.

I suggested to Aram, "Let's take our sleeping bags and go up late Saturday afternoon. We can check out the course before dark."

"Will you do the cooking?"

I nodded.

"Not beans and franks again?"

"Nope. I'll pop for a canned ham. And we can pick up some of that German potato salad and pumpernickel bread in Bismark, at Luden's delicatessen."

79

"You have just sold me," he said.

We weren't the only riders who wanted to check out the course. The parking lot was dotted with vans, campers, and pickups when we got there. We pulled in next to a Volkswagen van.

The hot amateur from Fresno was working on his Yamaha next to the van, and Dan Dunphy was helping him. I finally learned the amateur's name, when Dan introduced me. His name was Marty Kaprelian, and he was no longer an amateur.

He now had his card. He was, as I was, a probationary novice.

"I hate to say it in front of a Yamaha factory man," he told me, "but I think you and Gehrig have the fastest cycles in our class."

"Dan probably does, too," I said.

"No way!" Dan said. "Brad coming?"

"Yup. Have you guys run the course yet?"

Marty shook his head, and winked at me. "Why don't we let the old pro lead us around it?"

"I'll get my bike," Dunphy said, "and meet you at the starting line."

Line was the wrong word for it; it was a starting area, larger than the parking lot. A hundred bikes would be bunched here tomorrow, as the historic homesteaders had once assembled on their horses and in their wagons, awaiting the starter's signal.

Many desert meets are long and grinding all-day

affairs, attracting five or six hundred riders. This course was different, and so was the field, with a higher percentage of factory teams.

We would have a dead engine start tomorrow, but Dunphy was waiting for us, his engine idling, when Marty and I got there. This would not be a race. It was supposed to be a lesson.

There were only a few bikes working out, so no dust obscured our vision. Nine hundred feet above us, and three miles away, we could see the jagged outline of Calamity Rock, the turnaround point.

It was on a mesa. There would be about a quarter mile of level run up there. But from here to there, it was more hill climb than race. The return trip, along the northern slope, was a dangerous downhill and sidehill trail.

Marty and I followed Dan, taking our lesson. He didn't teach me a thing. Ahead of me, Marty, too, was not following the Dunphy line. It was plain to me we both knew this course better than Dan did. Why, then, had Marty suggested a lesson?

I asked him that, after Dan had gone back to his camper.

He smiled. "Did I use the word 'lesson'?"

"Maybe not. You're tricky, aren't you? You wanted to see where he made his mistakes, in case you tangled tomorrow. You've ridden this course often, haven't you?"

"I have. Did I do something wrong?"

"No more than I did. I watched your mistakes *and* Dan's. Do you like German potato salad?"

"Sure do. Do you like guitar music played by a semi-expert?"

To my inexpert ear, he was an expert. We ate the Danish ham, the German potato salad, the pumpernickel bread, and the kosher pickles. And then, around the fire, after the desert went from warm purple to cold, star-studded black, he played. A lot of the other boys gathered around to listen, comrades in arms—until tomorrow.

He was not a factory rider, but the Yamaha mechanics who came to service the Dunphys were working on Marty's bike, too, next morning.

"They can spot a winner," Aram said. "The Dunphys aren't getting any younger. What mistakes did he make yesterday?"

"None I noticed. I was only trying to psyche him."

"And *you* called *him* tricky?"

"Come on, Aram! It was all in fun!"

"Oh, yes," he said. "I forgot. This is Sunday. How do you want your eggs?"

"Edible," I said. "I'll do 'em."

The sun was hot overhead when we lined up; the promised overcast was missing. There were four lines of bikes stretched across the starting area. Brad was in the first line, your tricky narrator in the third. In front of all of us, there was a 500-yard stretch of rock-free, flat desert before we would dip down into the Devil's Arroyo.

Some of the bikes came to life on the second kick, some on the third. My Aram-tuned Oriole was one of the few that started on the first. I was through the line ahead and into the front row before I had to brake and downshift for the dip into the Devil's Arroyo.

There were two routes in and only one route out, all three of them one bike wide. I didn't count the machines ahead, as I funneled down, but I had to be in the upper quarter of the field, because this was the first line.

I picked my way between the larger rocks of the dry stream bed, riding the pegs to take the load off the suspension, skittering toward the steep and narrow climb out. I was a front-runner for only one reason: Aram's touch had given me the starting edge.

Two bikes in front went down before I came to the exit; there were less than a dozen bikes in front of me as I started up the bank.

Over the crest and out, into the rock- and cactus-dotted climb toward the mesa. Many of the bikes seemed to be in third, as we skimmed across the hard sand. The Oriole had enough torque to handle the grade in fourth, one ratio below the top.

A mile short of the peak, the sand grew softer and the climb steeper. I downshifted one notch and moved past the bike directly in front of me. The next challenge would be stiffer; Marty Kaprelian's Yamaha was now close enough to bounce grains of sand off my brand-new, tinted, safety-glass goggles.

It was too early to challenge. On our practice run yesterday, I had noticed how well he had handled the downhill trail, the second half of this course. I could use another lesson.

Near the bottom, the same stream bed we had ridden laterally on the way up cut directly across the trail. A ramp had been built by the Oasis City Cycle Club in front of the jump. Some wag had named it Loser's Leap. It had been put in last year; it was new to me.

It was not only a downhill jump, which is difficult enough. The landing area was also sidehill. It was the kind of leap that even mountain goats avoid, but Marty had flown it with a minimum of landing wobble yesterday. I wanted to see how he would handle it today.

I followed him up the slope to the rim of the mesa. Here, on the flat, hard sweep around Calamity Rock, he really turned it on. We went past three slower cycles before starting the downhill run.

The trail went right here, then left, in a long S curve, requiring a fine balance between braking and gassing, between ramming rocks or crashing cacti, between staying vertical or horizontal. The camber changed as the trail curved; the most delicate balance of all depended on shifting our weights precisely at the right moment.

The road swung left, toward the hill, as we approached the jump, but Marty rode the extreme right edge of it. I could understand his strategy; he was planning to jump *into* the hill at the landing area, his best hope for continuing traction.

I slowed, to give him room—and followed his example.

He was in the air, his front wheel lower than usual, when I gassed the Oriole before hitting the ramp. If he had gone down, I would have landed on top of him. He bounced hard twice, swung to the right—and I had room to land.

The shock of landing, even through the Oriole's stiff suspension, made my spine ache. I had taken too much of it on the rear wheel. But we were still up and running, and I had learned that downhill desert jumps are very different from artificial supercross jumps. At least they were different from the ones I had watched on the boob tube.

Down the winding, sidehill road to the pylon, Marty in front by almost a hundred feet now. Around the pylon, and Aram's board informed me I was riding sixth. I could see Joe's board, too, still in his hand. His board had informed Brad that he was riding third.

There were fifty-four miles to go. The temperature was in the low nineties. Inside my leathers, the temperature was higher. Sweat trickled down my legs and neck and sides, and fogged my goggles. Fifty-four more miles of this? Why? Believe it or not, it was still more fun than pumping gas or grinding valves.

Ahead of us was the flat, rock-free stretch. There was no way I could pick up enough ground in those five hundred yards to beat Marty to the arroyo. Patience, patience. . . .

I followed him into the arroyo. Brad was there, his cycle down. He lifted it and kicked it back into action as I moved around him. I was now riding fifth—with fifty-four miles (minus six hundred yards) still ahead of me.

I threaded between the rocks, a tinge of lower back pain lingering from the jump, a heavy overcast beginning to shroud the sun. The weatherman might be right, after all. It could stay cool—in the low nineties.

The Oriole was built of sterner stuff; she was feeling no pain, purring along, answering every summons without complaint or strain. Up and out, twenty feet behind Marty, veering slightly to the right, to avoid his dust. The three leading bikes were within range ahead, climbing the early, easier section of the slope toward the summit.

Marty made no move to close the gap. I followed his example. Riding in the first five among a hundred entries was higher than either of us had a right to expect. Though I did not plan to settle for fifth place—unless I had to.

Three laps later, I was almost ready to settle for it. Army Elkins had gone past in those three laps, and Don Dunphy. I was riding seventh. Two hundred feet ahead, Army was challenging Marty for fourth place.

In those three laps, I had tried the lower front-wheel jump technique and the ache in my back was less painful. I had passed at least a half-dozen bikes on their sides, but not one of them was among the leaders.

When Gary Park's Harley began to edge closer in the sixth lap, I decided enough was enough. It was time to become worthy of my mount.

Both of us zoomed past Don Dunphy, as we streaked the wide curve around Calamity Rock. We were too close, I realized, as we started down the hill. One of us would have to back off before the jump. That landing area was too small for both bikes.

I was still in front as we started down. Unless he passed me in the next two miles, the way I saw it, sportsmanship would demand that he back off. It might not be the way he saw it.

The Oriole didn't seem to be sharing my anxiety, snarling at the Harley. The Harley was snarling back, almost close enough to bite, as we swept through the long S curve.

Down the sidehill to the fairly flat area that led to the dip that led to the jump. The jump was now a quarter of a mile ahead. I could see Army Elkins and his Husky silhouetted against the gray sky as they soared over it.

I was an eighth of a mile from it when the snarl from behind grew dimmer. Gary was backing off. He was a sportsman. Harley-Davidson wouldn't be likely to hire anybody who wasn't.

The cynical second thought came to me that he must also have known that there wasn't room for two bikes on that landing ledge. I discarded that thought. Melvin T. was right; I was too young for cynicism.

Up, up, up and away—to my smoothest landing so far. Down the sidehill, those Kayden Sure-Grip Tires biting for traction, onto the flat and around the pylon.

Aram's board told me what I knew. I was riding sixth.

I had ridden fifth, then seventh, now sixth. In a field this size, that would qualify me a front-runner.

Winner has a richer ring to it, but trying too hard to be a winner could make me an also-ran.

I could no longer hear the snarl of Gary's Harley. A higher-pitched whine was coming up from behind, as I started the seventh lap. I concentrated on the trail ahead. The hill in front of me looked like a Christmas tree, ornamented with the glisten of fallen cycles. Looking back could make me one of the fallen.

As Satchel Paige so wisely said: *Never look back; something might be gaining on you.*

On the sharp turn after the arroyo, I didn't have to look back. Sideways was enough. Hans Nevel, the stormer, was creeping closer on his Marlowe.

That was one rider I didn't want too close when I came to the jump. He had been called many things by his friends and enemies. I was sure none of them had ever called him a sportsman.

Fly, Oriole, fly! Up the gradual grade to the steeper grade, to the softer sand. Dig, Kayden Sure-Grips, dig! I am too young to enjoy a showdown with Hans Nevel.

Over the crest and around the rock, Nevel trailing. The feeling grew in me that a showdown was certain. He planned to see if there was any chicken in this punk.

I didn't gain much down the slope, or through the S curve. But, as the jump loomed larger, the advantage was still mine. Unless he had a death wish, it was time to fall back.

The flat, the dip—and I gunned the Oriole for the ramp.

That crazy man! He had caught up, he was alongside, two feet to my right, as our bikes soared.

Something bitter came up from my stomach. I kept my eyes on the landing ledge and said a small prayer. I felt the rear wheel land, then the front. I was still upright.

Nevel wasn't. His bike had missed the right rim of the ledge. Both he and his machine were sliding down the hill, into the chaparral. The sand was soft there, and the cacti sparse.

He had taken a calculated risk on the safest place on the course to spill. The fact that his tactics might have curdled the blood of an innocent rookie had probably never entered his mind.

I was still sixth, with three laps to go. Nobody was challenging, nobody was within immediate range ahead, as I came out of the arroyo. A hundred yards past it, Army Elkins was trying to kick his Husky back into life. I was riding fifth.

It was a milk run from there in, the challengers too far behind to threaten, the leaders too far ahead to catch. In the ninth lap, Aram informed me I was riding fourth. That meant the second-place bike had gone down; I would have recognized the others.

That's where I finished, in fourth place.

"That lousy Nevel!" Aram said, as he handed me a Coke. "Should I go over and belt him one?"

I shook my head. "Let him lick his wounds in peace. He's had enough trouble for one day."

7

Brad had finished sixth, half a lap behind me. He had gone down three times. I thought going down three times and still finishing sixth was an accomplishment, which I told him.

"Finishing in the same lap as a desert fox like you is a bigger accomplishment," he said. "This really isn't my kind of going."

He was playing one-upmanship, but I didn't want to play. I said, "How about our brand-new novice, Marty Kaprelian? He finished second!"

"Marty's not brand-new to the desert, any more than you are."

I took a deep breath, and another swallow of Coke. "Brad, we're on the same team. Let's stop sniping at each other."

He looked down at the sand and up at Calamity Rock, and finally at me. He smiled wearily. "Okay.

Have you guys got any of that ham left? I could use a sandwich."

We finished the ham and pumpernickel bread and loaded the bikes and headed for home. A mile or so the other side of Oasis City, Aram said, "Didn't that give you the shakes when Nevel crowded you on the jump?"

"It sure did. But I had the safe side. His smart move would have been to come in on my left, force me to jump toward the rim. He's got a a lot of guts, but I'm not sure he's too bright."

"You were in the lead," Aram said. "The inside lane was yours. Maybe he respected that. Maybe he's not as bad as his reputation."

I shrugged.

He chuckled. "Brad was really down, wasn't he? You're starting to haunt him, again."

"Whatever that means."

"You know what I mean. Look at the record. And then, when he thinks it's all behind him, you show up on two wheels."

"Through the years," I said, "Brad Gehrig has beaten me almost as often as I've beaten him. If you'd have been his mechanic, he'd have beaten me more often."

"Probably. Although Joe's pretty good."

Nothing from me.

"I'm talking too much," he said. "I'm all wound

up and you're all wound down." He reached forward to snap on the radio. "I'll get us some soothing music."

Old Uncle Aram. . . . He deserved better company. But a jolting, hot and dusty sixty miles on two wheels had drained me. I was saddle sore and bone weary.

How did they do it? Those privateers in their battered vans, traveling from coast to coast, living on hot dogs and hamburgers, sleeping on a thin cushion over a steel floor, how did they do it?

Our way made more sense. We would meet the best at their best when they came to the west, and never be more than a night away from home cooking. Our way, it was still Sunday fun—most times.

Monday didn't give me any relief. Lee came to handle the drive and I helped Aram install new brakes in two cars, and a new differential in a truck. I went to bed at seven that night and slept for thirteen hours.

We would be at the Muldowney Raceway this Sunday. On the following Sunday, I would get my first test at motocross racing, at the Channing Ridge Roundup, near Sylvia.

Elkins had finally got his Husky going again at Oasis City, and finished ninth. He was now leading the national rankings for the year. He had been the

Pacific Coast leader last year and throughout most of this year.

Brad looked happier on Sunday. "Back to your kind of going?" I asked him.

"Come on, Sarge. We agreed—no sniping."

"I retract the question."

"I'm sorry about last Sunday," he said. "I'm a sour loser."

"Winners often are. Against the boys we're playing with, we're bound to lose our share."

"We shouldn't lose today. Elkins and his buddies are down at that hundred-miler in Phoenix."

"Brad," I said, "take a good look around you. Look at the boys here, and their bikes, and tell me again we shouldn't lose today."

"Okay. How about—we should do better today?"

"You have just earned yourself a triple whammy cheeseburger with a side order of coleslaw. Let's go."

Marty Kaprelian was over there, under the trees, eating with a man I recognized, the Yamaha dealer in Fresno. Aram and I had dickered with him when the original Oriole had collapsed. We got our food and sat down across from them.

"I'm being courted," Marty explained. "But I think I'll wait for an offer from Delta."

"You beat both Deltas at Oasis City," the dealer pointed out.

Marty winked at us. "I know. But on a Delta I'd have lapped 'em."

The dealer shrugged, finished his beer, wiped his mouth with the back of his hand, and stood up. "There are some other boys I have to see. Mike will be in your pit today." He nodded at us and went away.

"Who's Mike?" I asked.

"A Yamaha mechanic," Marty said. "That dumb remark about lapping you guys—I—"

"Will live to regret," Brad finished for him. "Yamaha wants you, huh?"

"Not the factory, only the local dealer. Marlowe has shown some interest, though. I guess they're getting ready to dump Nevel."

"That would be a mistake," Brad said. "I'm not in his fan club, but Hans Nevel is one heck of a competitor."

"You have just repeated what I told Marlowe. How come you hot-shoes aren't down at Phoenix?"

"We wanted a Sunday off," Brad explained. "We wanted some easy wins."

The pure amateur opener looked more professional today. They would get better and smarter and eventually make our lot harder.

In all trades, I guess, the young ones keep coming up, ready to take over your job. It was too early for me to complain about it; I was one of the young ones.

We were lucky in the draw. I had the third slot in

the first row, Brad the pole in the second row. I don't know where Marty started, but he was riding along with us front-runners by the time we hit the middle of the backstretch.

An old pro from Bakersfield was leading the parade at the time, on a gleaming new Harley. Brad was second, I third, a novice from Stockton fourth, and Marty fifth.

For six laps, we put on an interesting show, I thought, each of the leading characters fighting for the star's role, five competent and competitive professionals on our own stage.

And then, in the seventh lap, the hungry young tigers from behind began to move up, planning to turn it into the amateur hour.

Marty was the first victim, accepting the challenge of a wild kid on a matching Yamaha, forgetting his own sense of pace in the heat of the duel. Marty should have known they were hitting the grandstand turn too fast.

Both Yamahas went sliding up the bank, missing the fence by inches as half a dozen bikes moved past below.

The Stockton novice, riding in front of me, saw it happen, and learned nothing. He was the second victim as a kid on a sweet-sounding Husky tried to take him from the inside.

The Stockton rider had the groove and the right

to it. But he goosed his Suzuki and moved over, arrogantly confident the Husky didn't have the torque to take him.

He moved over just as I was starting to go by on the other side of him. That made me victim Number Three, as my front wheel hit his rear, as both bikes went into a shuddering gilhooley, as the Husky found room to gun past.

Neither of us went down. But Brad and the old pro were long gone and far away by the time we regained control. The Suzuki and the Delta fought it out for fourth place behind the amateur on the Husky. I edged past fifty feet short of the checkered flag.

Brad had won, half a length in front of the Harley, and I had taken a fourth. Two Deltas in the first four should make the factory happy. But not me.

"That punk from Stockton," I started to tell Aram, and then closed my mouth. The punk from Stockton was coming over.

"I'm sorry," he said. "That Husky was giving me so much trouble, I never even noticed you were going by."

"No harm, no foul," I said. "Forget it."

He held out a hand. "My name's Paul Wragge."

I shook his hand and said, "My name's Colin Sergenian. Most people call me Sarge."

"Don't be modest," he said. "I knew that. Everybody here knows you." He smiled, and went back to his pit.

"Nice kid," I said.

"That nice kid cost us about ninety bucks," Aram said. "Nice *arrogant* kid, if you ask me."

We all were, more or less. A Sunday off, some easy wins.... Brad already had one of them. "What happened to you?" he came over to ask.

I shrugged. Aram said, "He got tangled up with a nice kid. You looked great out there, Brad. Congratulations!"

"Thank you. Where did Marty finish?"

"Seventh. He met another nice kid."

Brad nodded. "I'm beginning to see the light. Amateurs, right? They'll put us all in the hospital."

"Only one was an amateur," Aram said. "The other should be."

"Let us not forget," I pointed out, "that this track was *built* by amateurs. And let us not forget that ancient racing tradition."

"What's that?" Brad asked.

"Winner buys the Cokes," I said. "Go get Joe. Aram and I will meet you at the snack bar."

It was at the snack bar that we learned what we would have learned if we had been here last Sunday. The third event, 250 cc's and under, would no longer be an open field. It was all professional today.

Most of the better local amateurs now had received their novice cards as pros. Melvin T. wouldn't need as many scorers if the amateurs were eliminated. The field had become too big and too complicated for a track this size.

"No amateurs in this one, thank heavens," Aram said.

Just the mean old pros, I thought, many of them over twenty, just the kids who never grew up.

Melvin T. had thought of another gimmick for the third event. Though some of the starting positions were determined by lot, those riders who had finished in the first eight in the previous race would start in the last row in this one. There was some grumbling in the last row and a frown on the face of Doc Kucera, but it was legitimate enough.

To the fans this seemed like fair play, giving the also-rans a better chance to earn some money. To Mr. Muldowney it seemed like smart showmanship, which it was.

Brad was back there, and the Bakersfield Harley, and Marty and Paul Wragge and yours truly, along with some others.

Next to me, Wragge said, "We can't complain. All we have in front of us are losers."

Aram was right again; he was an arrogant kid.

He could have had a second flaw, impatience. Heading into the first turn, he angled sharply for the

100

inner rail, the shortest route and a typical rookie mistake. He ran into the traffic jam there, swung wide to the right—and almost bumped into Brad, who was going past.

He swung back and was buried in the ruck as the back-liners made their early bids, high on the rim and going all out. Marty and I were dueling in the top third of the field before we came to the second turn. Brad was four bikes in front of us, within striking distance of the front row pair setting the pace.

Though he didn't have factory sponsorship, Marty's Yamaha was a well-tuned machine, a worthy opponent for the Oriole. We gained on the rest of the field, but not on each other.

We were only two bikes short of Brad at the end of the third lap. Brad was still chasing the front-row pair. If they were what Wragge had called losers, his dictionary was different from mine.

Our two-bike duel became a four-bike battle in the fifth lap. A pair of Monterey boys, one on a Triumph, the other on a Maico, were still between us and third place.

It might be unfair and too personal to say they were blocking the track. It would be fair to say they were determined to keep us back where we were—and it was a team effort.

When either Marty or I tried to pass them on the right, one of them shifted to the right. When we tried to go under them, the left-hand bike did the dirty work.

It wasn't until the seventh lap that we got some outside help. A lapper was chugging along in front of them, as we bored into the heavy dust of the north turn. They were so concerned with us that they didn't notice him in time.

When they did, they over-reacted, both of them hitting the brakes and cutting sharply up the grade. The rider on the left started his swerve too early. His Triumph rammed the Maico and both bikes went down.

They left a lot of track below. Marty and I went past and around the north turn, into the front lane. At the end of the straightaway, Brad had gone past the pair in front of him, and was entering the south. They were going past the pits as he disappeared around the turn.

Our chances of catching Brad in three laps were slim, thanks to the pair from Monterey. But those two a quarter of a lap ahead were still within reach. Marty and I took off.

Give us an E for effort. We picked up all but ten feet of their quarter-lap lead. Make it nine feet for the Delta. I edged out Marty by a foot, to take fourth place.

Twice in one day, Delta had finished in the top four. I should have been happier than I was.

8

Pacific Division points were to be earned by the first eight riders to finish. The pair from Monterey had finished sixth and seventh—or so they thought, until Doc Kucera came on the PA system to announce that both of them had been disqualified for "unsportsmanlike interference with the progress of other entrants."

That made me a little less gloomy. And then Brad came over to say, "The creeps! You and I could have put on a real show for the folks if it hadn't been for them."

"Thank you, sir. And congratulations. You called it and you did it—two easy wins."

He smiled. "But there's always tomorrow, isn't there?"

I nodded.

He really hadn't meant tomorrow, only figuratively. But it made him an accurate prophet twice that afternoon. Because Monday was the day Berjouhi got her letter of acceptance from Stanford. My bright and sassy sister was going to be a "collitch" kid.

The folks had been disappointed when I had decided to go into business with Aram, instead of to college. Judged by our comparative scholastic records, I had more need of it than she did. But she could put it to better use. Horses for courses is the way I saw it.

I'm not about to downgrade the worth of a college education. But if you just can't afford it, remember this: There is very little a college can teach you that you can't learn for yourself in your local public library.

Dykstra came over from San Jose on Wednesday, bringing some spare parts for both bikes, and some Cunningham tires for the Channing Ridge Roundup.

There would be more jumps at Channing Ridge. There would be water, and whoop-de-doos and sharper rocks. Cunninghams were better designed for that kind of going than the Kaydens.

"Let me say while I'm here," Dykstra told us, "how pleased both Mr. Loft and I are with the job you two and the Gehrigs have done for Delta. And let me add that we are fully aware that neither you, Sarge, nor Brad, has had much experience at motocross racing. But you did very well at Oasis City, and that's roughly the same type of race."

"I hope so," I said. "It's been bothering me."

"Don't let it. We're not expecting a miracle."

"What did he mean by a miracle?" Aram asked me, when Dykstra had left. "Like maybe twentieth?"

"Maybe finishing in one piece," I said. "He's right, though. That race at Oasis City was more motocross than desert scramble."

Aram shrugged. "We'll see."

We saw, on Saturday afternoon. We saw trees that were both thick and close together. We saw a stream that meandered across the trail, with some rocks sharp enough to rip a tire, some big enough to crumple a tank.

We didn't like what we saw—but it was an interesting challenge.

The big boys would all be here, with a chance to win both Pacific and National points, plus, of course, some money.

Brad and Joe arrived as we were unloading the bike. "Ever run this course?" I asked Brad.

He nodded. "Twice. It's mean, Sarge. We'll do well to finish."

I'd had three consecutive fourth-place finishes on the last two Sundays, and now would do well to finish at all. It was still an interesting challenge.

"Let's try it," I said. "You lead the way."

"Okay," he said. "Keep it in third."

There were several places where a rider could turn it on, but this was an inspection trip. We loafed through it, mostly in third or fourth gear. We crossed the stream eight times, four times as a jump, four times on wet wheels. We threaded between rocks and trees where there was no room to pass, and finished with a half mile flat stretch of grass tufts and hard ground as wide and clear as a deserted freeway.

We ran the course two more times, and took the last half mile all out in fifth gear on the final trip. We started roughly even in that spurt—and I finished well ahead of Brad. The bikes were identical, but not the mechs.

The sun was low in the west when we got back to our camping ground. Joe and Aram had started the fire, and were talking with Army Elkins.

"I understand," Army said to Brad, "that you took advantage of my absence from Muldowney last Sunday. Two wins?"

Brad nodded.

"The big companies will be after you before long," Army said.

Brad smiled. "If we keep winning, maybe the big companies will have to put out quality cycles, too."

"Ouch!" Army said. He grinned. "See you tomorrow, boys."

"That was a great line," I told Brad. "The part I liked was where you said, 'if *we* keep winning.' "

"You'll win your share before this year is over. We both know that, Sarge. Let's eat."

Aram had brought some food from home, cabbage *sarma* and cheese *bearegs, sou-bearegi* with *madzoon.* We were eating all-Armenian tonight.

The hungry looks Joe and Brad gave us as they munched their hamburgers finally broke down our resistance. We shared our delicacies with them, 70-30. Thirty percent seemed a fair share for men already well stuffed with hamburger.

There would be two heats tomorrow, the first in the morning, the second in the afternoon. A two-heat average would decide the winner.

The course was about three and a half miles long, so two ten-lap heats would make it a seventy-mile day. That was ten miles longer than the desert run that had drained me. But we would have a rest and a lunch between heats, and a temperature in the low seventies.

It was a cold and moonless night, possibly the reason for the black thoughts I had. I couldn't sleep, thinking about tomorrow.

Even before the last two Sundays, I'd finished too often in fourth place. Against the headliners, fourth. Against the newcomers, fourth. What a silly pattern. Ladies and gentlemen, we present to you on his brand new Delta Oriole—Fourth Place Sergenian!

On that hard, flat stretch before the finish line, my machine had proven to be faster than Brad's. And he had come through with two wins for Delta last week. But remember, Colin, you finished ahead of him on a course much like this one. Keep that thought in mind and get to sleep. . . .

In the morning, Aram said, "You were doing a lot of mumbling last night."

"I couldn't fall asleep."

"Great! How are you going to feel seventy miles from now?"

I shrugged.

He studied me. "We don't have to run, you know. We can go home."

"I'll be all right! Once I get some food in me, I'll be all right."

Two eggs and three strips of bacon later, I wasn't all right, but I was closer to it.

Aram had been quiet while we ate. Now, he said, "It's Brad, isn't it? You make everything too personal."

"It's not completely personal. I'm not doing the job for Delta that I should."

"Baloney! Dykstra's happy with the job you're doing. It's personal. And remember this, feisty—if you push yourself too far, you can wind up in intensive care."

I didn't have a chance to argue with him; Joe and Brad were coming from their camper.

Brad smiled and said, "Your turn today, Sarge. Your kind of track." He paused. "You look tired."

Tired of fourth place, I thought. I said, "I'll be okay."

I did their eggs for them. Four grown men, and I was the only one who could do justice to an egg. Eggs have to be treated tenderly, like a small man's ego.

There would be sixty-five bikes in the Roundup, most of them carrying men and boys out for a little Sunday fun. The others were riders seeking points and money, of which I was one.

Fifty yards beyond the gate, the whoop-de-doos started. There was a long flat stretch beyond them, followed by a sweeping curve that straightened out before the first jump.

The lottery had put me roughly in the center of the field. Halfway down the flat stretch, the man with the sign was waiting for the signal to flip it to two minutes. When it reached one minute, I would start my count. Ten seconds before the gate opened, I would put my bike in gear.

That's what I did—and so did everybody else. Sixty-five chattering bikes stampeded toward the gate, every rider looking for a hole.

I hadn't had much experience with whoop-de-doos. The little I'd had convinced me the best way to overcome their corduroy-road effect was to take them fast, skimming over the ridges, not allowing the suspension enough time to bottom.

About half of the riders in front of me tried the opposite technique. I went past six of them before I came to the flat stretch.

Top gear here, and down to fourth for the long curve. I couldn't estimate how many bikes were ahead, because of the dust, but I had to be six positions higher than I had started.

The jumps on this course were shorter and less risky than the Losers' Leap at Oasis City. I braked before the first, then fed the Oriole only enough birdseed to clear without soaring. On this course, time in the air was lost time.

A sharp turn followed the jump. I rode inside the berm to the fast straight track ahead. There would be a wet crossing at the end of it, and some of the riders downshifted early as I sailed past. A hundred yards short of the crossing, I jammed both binders, downshifted, and eased into the water.

There was a Marlowe stopped, its ignition swamped, that I had to swerve around before climbing the gravel path to the far bank of the stream. Onward and upward, the dark night behind me.

I threaded beween the rocks and skinned between the trees, up a gradual rise to another jump. Over

I went, landing with the back brake gently dragging, to bring that front wheel down before the hairpin turn around the pivot pole that marked the turn-around point.

I bobbed along a straight and bumpy stretch to the next wet crossing, and came out onto a long curve on a slight downslope where a rider could turn it on—before the next jump.

I used my first water-crossing technique here, as the Maico in front of me downshifted early. I streaked past him in fifth gear, before I hit both brakes, and then goosed the Oriole lightly for the takeoff.

I was in the trees once more, the footing underneath slippery with fallen leaves, the gloomy shade stirring the dark memory of last night. The traction grew better, and so did my mood, as I came out into the sunlight again and into the immediate, high-speed now of hairline judgments about which clusters of rocks were safest to get through.

I sneaked past them all, leaving the hazards behind, as I upshifted for the flat, hard, go-for-broke last half mile. There were a dozen bikes in sight between me and the finish line. I couldn't be any higher than thirteenth.

I passed three of the bikes before the end of the lap. I was riding tenth, Aram informed me. Under the "10" he had chalked an "E-Z!" That screeching half mile must have had him thinking I was still making it personal.

I was, but it was a personal competition against myself. I had gone from the middle of the field to the upper sixth without strain. With a little extra effort in the next nine laps—why not dream high?

One of the reasons is the company you are forced to keep. When you dream high, you run into a lot of winners. The first one I encountered was Gary Park on his Harley.

He was spinning along the fast stretch before the first water crossing when I came up from behind. He didn't use the rookies' technique; he used the one I had chosen—all out and hit the brakes.

Either the Oriole's brakes were better, or its recovery faster. Whatever, I led him into the stream, and out of it.

Between the rocks, the slight upgrade, the sound from behind growing dimmer, the Marlowe ahead looming larger. Hans Nevel was leaving the rocks and heading into the woods when I moved up on his right.

I didn't beat him; he beat himself. The hell-for-leather technique that had earned him his nickname was not designed for narrow passages. His Marlowe was a sturdy machine, but not nearly as sturdy as the live oak it rammed. He was staring down at a crushed front wheel as I slipped past.

Over the jump I leaped, and into the hairpin, around it, around the pole, and down into the water. Back to fourth gear for the long curve that led to the next jump.

A Yamaha twin, either Dan or Don, was moving briskly twenty-five yards in front. I couldn't identify him from behind.

Old pros take it easy through the early laps of long races. As we drew even, I saw it was Dan, Don's identical twin, except for the moustache. We took the jump together.

We stayed even along the stretch that led to the next wet crossing. We moved carefully through the stream, side by side. Coming out, and edging between the trees, I didn't crowd the Oriole. My advantage was still in front.

Two crossings later, the advantage opened, one-half mile of top-gear speed. So long, Dan Dunphy.

It would be exciting to relate how I fought it out with each of the six riders still in front of us. Climbing from seventh place at the end of the second lap to the ultimate encounter with the champ in the last lap is the stuff that dreams are made of.

It was less spectacular than that. Most of the bikes I sailed past were either bent or wet. The course had been my ally.

Elkins had led through the last four laps. I hadn't even seen him until I climbed out of the water after the hairpin. His Husky was just going around the bend in front of the first downgrade jump.

I didn't try to pull even, as I had with Dunphy. I trailed, never close enough to threaten, never far enough behind to make my strategy hopeless.

He knew I was there. He must have felt certain that if I was still there when we came to that final half mile, the Husky would be a cinch to outrun the Oriole.

I was still there, ten yards behind him, when we hit payoff alley. Halfway through that stretch run, the Husky was well behind me. I didn't look back after that, but Aram told me I had finished at least fifty yards in front.

Mr. Number One was the first of the riders to congratulate me. For a man who had so little practice at losing, he certainly handled it well.

"You finally have a bike to match you," he told me. "When my Husqvarna contract expires, I may take a trip to San Jose."

"I'm sure they'd love to have you at Delta," I said. "But they can't afford a champion, not yet. They're on a *very* limited budget."

He smiled. "Funny fellow! We'll meet again, you and I."

I smiled back at him. "That's what I'm afraid of."

Brad had finished eighth, Marty Kaprelian fifth, Paul Wragge twelfth. Two Deltas had finished in the first ten, one Husky, one Harley, two Suzukis—and *four* Yamahas.

That looked great for Yamaha, until broken down. There had been thirteen Yamahas entered, and only two Deltas. It was possible that a few more stars would now be traveling to San Jose when their contracts ran out.

The morning weariness came back during lunch. It was also partly an emotional letdown, after thirty-five miles of tension. The morning sense of gloom didn't come back with it; it was pure fatigue.

Aram said, "We've still got an hour and a half before the second heat. Why don't you take a nap?"

"Do I look that tired?"

He nodded.

I tried to take a nap. I lay down on a blanket over the soft grass in the shadow of the pickup. But there was yacking all around me, and engines revving, and the second heat still to come. There was no way I could fall asleep.

Do not read the above as an alibi. I have no reason to need an alibi for my performance in the second heat. Luck was involved, but it was both good and bad. And I'm sure there were plenty of other riders who'd had trouble sleeping the night before.

I started in almost the same middle of the pack as I had in the first heat. But the riders in front handled the whoop-de-doos better this time. I had passed half a dozen of them the first time around through this stretch. I managed to get by only two of them this time.

On the first water crossing, some wild kid on a Kawasaki came splashing in next to me like a crippled whale. His ignition died, and he went down. The Oriole's ignition faltered, almost died, but sputtered back to life as I started through the trees. Three bikes went past as it was sputtering.

Losing three places could be called bad luck; recovering from the splashed ignition balanced it. Dropping three places this early in the race could hardly be called a calamity.

I had the three places back and four more by the end of the second lap. I was not zinging, as I had in the opening heat; my bike and I were moving with the calm, if weary, assurance of a team that had recently finished first.

Army Elkins had been buried in the ruck at the start. He came charging up from behind in the third lap. *We'll meet again, you and I.*

He went past as we skirted the pylon. I didn't try to chase him. It might not happen today, but we would meet again.

In the sixth lap, Marty Kaprelian's Yamaha had gone down between two rocks, blocking a passage I had planned to take. I found another, shorter and firmer. Marty's bad luck had been my good luck; the shorter route brought me out ahead of the bike in front of him.

That is the way it went. Let me summarize it for you with the tally sheet from the scorers' table:

RIDER	MACHINE	FIRST HEAT	SECOND HEAT	AVERAGE	FINISH
Elkins	Husqvarna	2nd	1st	1½	First
Park	Harley-Davidson	4th	2nd	3	Second
Dan Dunphy	Yamaha	3rd	5th	4	Third
Sergenian	Delta	1st	8th	4½	Fourth

Fourth-place Sergenian had finished fourth once more. But it didn't depress me, not after I had gone head to head with Mr. Number One in that final lap —and beaten him.

9

In a properly compensated analysis, Marty Kaprelian could be considered the day's overall winner. Nine of the first ten places had been won by factory riders. Marty had finished tenth, half a point behind Brad, who had finished ninth.

On a works machine, expertly tuned and factory modified for the course, it was logical to assume he would have finished higher. Among the western privateers, he was the most consistent high finisher. And this was his rookie year.

"If we had him, too," I told Aram on the drive home, "Delta would be in great shape."

"The heck with that," Aram said. "We don't need three Delta dealers in the Fresno area. We and the Gehrigs are enough."

Nothing from me.

"Don't give me any of that merchant-thinking jazz, either," he said.

"The thought never entered my weary brain," I said. "I like that guy, though."

"You should like Brad, too, today. You creamed him."

"I have *always* liked Brad, since the day we first met. I'll lay off the merchant jazz, if you stop knifing me about Brad."

"It's a deal. Hey, you took Mr. Big today in the stretch run!"

"But he took first overall."

"That's why he's Mr. Big," Aram said. "Patience, partner."

Monday turned hot and Tuesday hotter. If it kept up, riding the Muldowney Raceway would be like riding the rim of an active volcano.

Melvin T. had a portion of the stands already covered. For a slight increase in admission, the luckier spectators could sit in the shade. As for us, he knew we would be there, shade or sun.

On Wednesday, the *Coast Cycle Weekly* finally had fourth-place Sergenian listed in the Pacific Top Twenty. I was fifteenth, thanks to my showing at Channing Ridge, where I had picked up ten points in the first heat and three in the second.

Brad had been ranked twelfth after his two wins at Muldowney the week before. The five points he had earned at Channing Ridge had not advanced him; he was still twelfth.

Among the first ten in the Pacific listing, six of the riders also held rankings on the National list. We'll-meet-again Elkins led both lists. But the king would be making the important eastern meets to preserve his National crown. We peasants should profit by his absence.

The heat held through Friday night, cooled off some on Saturday, and was down to 94° on Sunday, under a heavy overcast. In the San Joaquin Valley, that is called a temperate summer day.

I had half-planned to wear heavy jeans instead of my leathers, but Papa Aram put the no-no on that. They would be almost as hot, he explained, and not nearly as protective. If I had gone into that bramble bush protected only by jeans. . . .

Both the covered and uncovered sections of the stands were starting to fill up when we got to the track. We had hardy fans. Melvin T. had trucked an ice chest over to the pits and was doling out free orange juice to all the racing personnel.

"My favorite semi-Armenian," he said, as he handed me a sixteen-ounce mug of orange juice. "You made me proud at Channing Ridge, Colin."

I nodded toward the filling stands. "And rich here."

"*Aagh!*" he said. "You—"

"Mr. Muldowney," I said, "thank you."

"You're welcome. I've been thinking, Sarge,

maybe next year you'd like to hit the national trail. I could—"

"No," I said. "It's not for me. I guess I'm just a country boy, Mr. Muldowney."

He nodded. "I understand. You're not going to believe me, but so am I."

"I believe you. City boys don't wear ten gallon hats."

"Get out of here," he said. "You're holding up the line."

Elkins, Dan Dunphy, and Gary Park would be at the Denver hundred-miler today. Don Dunphy had stayed behind. He was not having as successful a season as his brother was; splitting the team could win Yamaha both National and Pacific points today. California was *the* major market for motorcycles.

Hans Nevel and some of the Marlowe privateers were in Nevel's pit, clustered around a tall young man in civvies.

"Who's he?" I asked Aram.

"A writer for *Cycle World.* He's the one who wrote that nasty piece about Hans in this month's issue."

"He's got a lot of guts, showing up here."

"He probably thought Hans would be in Denver."

"I wonder why he isn't?"

Aram smiled. "He'd rather play with the pigeons than the hawks."

We were by no means pigeons, more like fledgling hawks. And scattered through the aviary were a number of mature and sharp-clawed eagles.

Melvin T. was sauntering over to Nevel's pit now, 250 pounds of peacemaker. The privateers went back to their pits, and the writer went over to talk with Marty Kaprelian, *Cycle World*'s Rookie of the Month.

A steady breeze from the Sierras was lifting little whirlpools of dust from the barren spots in the infield. If it kept up, it might drop the temperature to 92° by midnight.

The cowboys were getting ready for the curtain raiser. Doc Kucera was lecturing one of them, probably for some shenanigans we had missed seeing last week. The ranch hands in the stands let Doc know he was scolding one of their idols.

They put on a first-class show, a little short on finesse, maybe, but full of daring, dust, and a disdain for disaster. All of them were running home-modified street machines, and most of them were top-level haywire mechanics. They had those assembly-line products singing high soprano.

A pup tent would have covered the first four finishers. If I hadn't known them personally, how competitive they were, and how honest, I would have sworn they had staged a hippodrome finish.

Their people gave them a standing ovation as they idled into the pits.

"I wonder where the Gehrigs are?" Aram said. "They didn't go to Denver, did they?"

I shook my head. "I talked with Brad on the phone Monday. He said something about a family wedding they were supposed to go to, but were trying to get out of. I guess they got stuck."

"That leaves it up to us," Aram said. "Go out and defend the honorable name of Delta."

Dumbest thing, it seemed strange without Brad out there. Through the years, he had been my measuring stick. In the karts, in the drags, we had shared many firsts and as many seconds. I know the only sensible strategy is to compete against yourself, but Brad's consistent excellence had given me a ruler with which I could measure myself.

Brad's absence had not left me short of measuring sticks. In the front row, I was flanked by Yamahas, Don Dunphy on the right, Marty on the left. To the left of Marty, Paul Wragge had the pole.

Very few riders can invade the shadow area of a false start with more precision than Don Dunphy. But the anticipation of the Stockton rookie on his Suzuki edged all of us today. Paul Wragge was off and running, heading the field into the first turn.

Don, possibly annoyed at getting beat at his own

game, went gassing after him, too fast and too soon. Marty and I played it cooler; we moved toward the inner rail as Don went sliding up the bank.

We stayed there, haunting Paul, all the way through the first lap. Nobody was closing in from behind; we continued to follow our leader, never letting him get out of challenging range. One of the better ways to stay vertical is to stick with a pace no faster than enough to keep you in contention.

The way I saw it, and probably Marty did too, there was no reason to overplay a winning hand too early in the game. When showdown time came, we had no doubt we could handle the raw rookie from Stockton.

Somewhere in the middle laps, I realized that Marty and I were following the same arrogant reasoning as the kid we were chasing. Paul, too, was not overplaying what he had to consider a winning hand. So long as we were content to stay behind him, why crowd the Suzuki?

I gave him reason in the sixth lap, making a sudden charge in the backstretch, hoping to startle him into taking the north turn too fast and too wide.

He didn't panic, riding well below the berm and finding a firm route into the grandstand stretch. I went into the turn faster and higher, and came out with a straighter, if softer, line down the grade.

The Oriole came digging out of the loose footing

without wavering or losing ground. I went past Wragge before we were past the pits, into first place, stretching the daylight between us.

From there to the middle of the final lap, it was like a time trial, unchallenged, running free. Don Dunphy moved up then to make it a contest, trying to pass outside in the backstretch, to get by inside through the turn.

He made it close, but never scary. I came out of the grandstand bend five feet in front of him and led him all the way to the checkered flag.

Two wins on consecutive Sundays. I no longer missed Brad quite as much as a true friend should.

"Ace!" Aram said.

"And another ace in the hole," I said. "You. Who can beat a pair of aces?"

He smiled. "The three kings in Denver, maybe?" He lifted his hand, palm toward me, to stop my reply. "A little joke, Sarge, just a little joke."

A little joke—with enough truth in it to give it bite. At Channing Ridge, the three kings had topped the pair of aces. But not every hand, I reminded myself; the aces had taken the first pot.

"So I'll have to get better," I said.

"That's our third ace," he said. "You're getting better every time out."

He spoke a near truth. I was getting better, but not *every* time. In baseball, at the plate, you can go

125

one for twenty, hit a streak and go ten for twelve. In golf, you can rim seven putts in one round, drop all seven on the next round, with the same stroke. In tennis, there are days when every call goes against you, days when every call is in your favor. Losers like to write the bad days off as bad luck.

In motorcycle racing, there are those bad times that you zigged when you should have zagged.

The third feature of the afternoon at Muldowney was one of those unlucky times. Bad luck can be an alibi for bad judgment. I'll admit I was guilty of bad judgment; but also I was a victim of bad luck.

My first mistake was the same one Dunphy had made in the second race. We were back to the lottery this week. It had put me in the first row again, along with Hans Nevel, Marty, and Don.

The charge still sizzling in me from my win had made me overanxious. As Don had, I charged that first turn as though it were a final stretch-run decider.

Three bikes had gone past Don when he had slid up the bank. The entire field swept past below as I fought to keep the Oriole from crashing the upper rail. In the first 150 yards of an 8800-yard race, I had gone from the third slot of the front row to dead last.

There were now twenty-three bikes in front of me, more mountain than a sensible man could expect to climb. My judgment error was trying to reach the peak. With the Oriole under me, I knew I was going to climb.

I climbed without trying in the first lap. A Marlowe had gone down, high on the bank of the second turn. I went past a sputtering Maico before the lap was completed.

On the far turn of the second lap, a Harley rider from Ventura made progress more difficult. He had left a hole below halfway through the turn, taking it high for a straighter line into the backstretch.

He came gunning down the slope as I shot for the opening. He was still in front. The hole was closed. I had to hit both brakes and downshift fast to keep the engine running. That had to be called an error in judgment; his planned route had been clear enough.

The Oriole made up for my lack, streaking the backstretch like a rocket, flying past the Harley before reaching the next turn.

Traffic kept getting heavier as I kept moving up. In the fifth lap, Aram's board didn't have my numerical position. He knew I wasn't interested in a statistic that depressing. The board held a simple fraction—"½." I was one-half lap behind the leader.

My dumbest move of the day came in the ninth lap. After fighting through all the crowded traffic behind, I finally came within sight of the leaders,

Hans, Marty, and Don. I was running fourth at the time, and though they were within sight, even Don Quixote would not have considered them within reach.

With my bad start, a fourth would have been a highly respectable finish. With my second-race win, it would have added up to a high-point afternoon.

Maybe it was my fourth-place hangup that was partly responsible. Whatever, I twisted the Oriole into the red zone and took out after the unreachable.

The three in front were throwing up a solid cloud of dust as they dueled for the lead. In that dust, a lapper was limping along, taking up a lot of track on an ancient Temple.

The track he was taking up when I saw him was the track directly in front of me. At our relative speeds, the only way to go was up, and nothing to stop me there except the fence.

I managed to stop short of the fence—as half a dozen bikes I had passed, plus the lapper, went spinning on their way to the flag.

We know you don't like fourth place, Sergenian. Why don't you try for eleventh?

That is where I finished.

10

"Rotten luck," Aram said. "You almost did it, buddy. You came from a long way back."

"I had fourth place cinched!"

He smiled. "We have enough of those. I admire a man who dreams the impossible dream."

"Even if it doesn't come true?"

He nodded. "What a sorry thing a fact is, measured against a dream."

I stared at him.

"A quote from my Uncle Nazar, the unpublished poet," he explained. "We had a fine day, ace. I'm proud of you. Let's get the truck loaded and get out of here before those heavyweights start throwing dust."

About halfway home, he asked, "Why so quiet?"

"I've been thinking. On the way out there, I would have been happy if I'd known I was going to come through with a win."

"Yup. You often expect too much from yourself, Sarge."

"And then, after that, I was thinking, if Brad had been there, and Elkins and Park and Dunphy, I probably wouldn't have won."

"Yes, you would. Today, you would have. You were hot! If you're asking me if, day in and day out, you're as good as Elkins, the answer is no. Did you expect to be, your first pro year?"

"Not when I started, but maybe now. That's really dumb, isn't it?"

He laughed. "Not for you. To re-quote my unpublished uncle, stick with the dream. Hardly anybody in the world is as good as he thinks he is. Why should you be an exception?"

"You are, Aram. You're as good as you think you are. Maybe better."

"I know," he said, grinning. "But how many do you find like me?"

There couldn't be many. I never had found any. All those trophies I had won because of him. He had none. They also serve who only stand and wait—in the pits.

Aram didn't need trophies or a measuring stick. He knew who he was and what he was and how good he was at what he did.

Wednesday's *Coast Cycle Weekly* had me listed thirteenth in the Division, six points behind Brad, still twelfth. If I had played it cool in that third race, I would have picked up seven more points and jumped to eleventh place, one point in front of Brad.

Compete only with yourself, as your father told you, Colin. I'll try, Papa, but it's not easy.

On Thursday, I learned in the society section of the *Fresno Bee* that I was not the only over-competitive member of the Delta racing team. The so-called "family" wedding Brad and Joe had been *forced* to attend last Sunday had been the wedding of their sister.

We would have two consecutive Sundays away from the heat of the San Joaquin Valley. This Sunday, we would travel up the coast to Seacliff for fifty miles of roller-coaster dunes and forest trail. The National headliners wouldn't be there; they would be in Houston, at the Astrodome supercross.

The biggie on the following Sunday would bring us all together again, one hundred miles of top-gear going on the mile-long paved oval at Valdesto Pines.

We would need another set of tires for that one; knobbies on that surface at those speeds would shake our teeth loose.

"That Valdesto run could prove something, I believe," Aram said.

"What's that?"

"I think this Oriole tops out higher than any 125 in the world."

"If I can keep it vertical."

"You will. Just remember it will be a mixed field. Don't try to take on any of the big bikes."

"Not unless they get in the way," I said.

Seacliff, as you must have guessed, is near the sea. But there is no cliff in the area worthy of the name. There is a hilly section of timber above the bumpy dunes; three-quarters of the course is a trail through the trees. The other quarter is sand, hard packed in the ridges, soft at the crests, about a hundred yards inland from the sea.

There were flags to mark the beach route, laid out in patterns like a ski run. They were wide enough apart to give a rider some leeway in his choices. The shorter routes were softer, the packed routes faster. It would take a precise sense of pace and alert steering to run the fast route, threading between the dunes.

Many of the gang were there when we got to Seacliff on Saturday afternoon. Marty Kaprelian was tuning his guitar when we pulled in next to him at the campground. He came over to help us unload.

"Why aren't you out there practicing?" I asked him. "Or have you been here all week?"

"I got here half an hour ago," he said. "Why

practice? I know this course like the back of my hand. I'll run you through it, if you want."

"Maybe, after we eat. Is Brad here?"

He nodded. "He's running the course. He's been here for two days. Did you bring some more of that German potato salad?"

I shook my head. "We're back to hamburger. Congratulations on your win last week."

"Thank you. Same to you. Can you imagine that Brad thinking one dumb race is more important than his own sister's wedding? Joe really read him the riot act about that."

"Joe's a mechanic," I explained. "They're not as kookie as riders."

"Amen," Aram said. "Get those hamburgers started. I'll finish the unloading."

Joe came over while we were eating. "Partners!" he said. "Congratulations on your win last week, Sarge."

"Thank you. Where's Brad?"

"Three guesses. We've been here since Thursday, but it wasn't my idea." He paused. "You know what his excuse was? He doesn't think he's doing the job for Delta that he should."

Aram smiled, and said nothing. I said nothing, without smiling.

"What I came over for," Joe said, "was some brake pads. Got any extras? Brad's hard on brakes."

133

"So is Sarge," Aram said. "I've got a million of 'em, partner."

Brad was still out there when Marty led me on his guided tour. Most of his lines through the forest were the same ones I would have taken. On the outgoing jump over the arroyo that split the woods, on the return jump over the same arroyo, we handled both about the same.

It was on the lines through the sand where we differed. He loved those hummocks, bouncing from crest to crest like a kid on a trampoline, his rear wheel spouting a fantail of sand. I followed his example on our first trip, found my own firmer line on the next three.

I would have taken him every time on the longer route if I hadn't slowed down before climbing back to the hard surface at the end of it.

"Well?" he said, when we'd finished.

"The way you handled those dunes," I said. "Why the showboating? Going around them is faster."

"Maybe. But not as much fun. Remember, Sarge, I'm not a factory rider. I don't *have* to win."

"I know. Are you telling me you're not going to try to win tomorrow?"

He stared at me. "Of course I'm going to try! That was a joke, Sarge! If I ever get the right offer, I'll be a factory man myself."

"Sorry," I said. "I've been edgy lately."

"Brad, too," he said. "And for no reason. Both of you must know that Delta's happy with you. Cool it, kid! Tonight, I'll play you some soothing music on my *gee-*tar."

He wasn't the only amateur musician at the meet. We had a quartet that night, a harmonica, a fiddle, an accordion, and Marty's guitar, country boys playing sweet country corn and singing sad cowboy laments.

I slept better than I had at Channing Ridge. Waves washing on a shore are a great soporific. Aram had the coffee made before I woke, and was waiting patiently for me to do the eggs.

"You look more chipper," he said. "Was it the music, or is it the scenery?"

"I guess it was Marty. We don't *have* to be here, do we?"

"Oh, yes, we do. We have to keep Delta solvent. I want that dealership."

"Two riders and two mechs can't keep Delta solvent."

"Don't be so sure. Dykstra told me orders have been picking up since you and Brad got hot."

I had half-planned to get in a few more runs before the course was closed to practice that morning, but Aram thought our time would be better spent splashing around in the ocean.

Most of the other riders and mechs seemed to

share Aram's thought. The National rankers were in Houston; this was the group that still believed in Sunday fun.

There would be forty-eight of us fighting for fame, points, and money through ten laps of a five-mile course. At least twenty of them must have known that their chance to win any of the three was somewhere between remote and impossible.

What a sorry thing a fact is, measured against a dream. . . .

I were lucky in the lottery, well up toward the front of the field. And what should be paired next to me but a skinny kid on a new Delta, a street Oriole, obviously home-modified.

He looked over and grinned. "You don't know me," he said, "but I've been to your filling station a couple of times. You're Sarge Sergenian, aren't you?"

"Right. How come we never met? I usually work the drive."

"I always came on Sunday. My name is Jess Kowalski. I tried to buy your old bike."

I had finally met the kid from Clovis. "You bought the right bike," I said. "Luck, Jess."

"Thanks. I'll need it, to keep up the payments. These Deltas aren't cheap, are they?"

"Not in any way," I said.

It was a dead-engine start. Both of our engines

started on the first kick. Fourth-place Sergenian and the kid from Clovis were in the top five by the time we reached the end of the long macadam strip that led into the woods.

The trail narrowed at the end of the macadam into a one-bike width between two second-growth redwood trees. All five of us filed in without fuss or challenge, two Harleys and a Suzuki in front of me, Jess directly behind.

This part of the trail had been a logging road originally, packed hard enough for fourth-gear speeds. The five of us went scooting along, all of us content to stay where we were for the moment.

Fifty yards short of the logging-road bridge, the course veered off toward the first jump. There was a long **S** curve over bumpy ground before the jump; I downshifted into third.

The two Harleys cleared the jump without trouble. The rider on the Suzuki got his front wheel too low, bounced sideways when he landed, and went sliding into the brush.

Another **S** curve followed the jump, a hairpin turn followed that. I went to fourth gear on the curves, back to third for the hairpin. At the turnaround point, Jess Kowalski still trailed, both Harleys still led.

There was a straight, hard stretch ahead before the second jump. The urge was strong in me to take the Harleys there and then. But the rider on the lead machine was considered one of the best in the West on sand; I wanted to watch his technique on the dune run.

Over the arroyo with no jar, back to the same bumpy surface we had traveled before the first jump. Behind me, Jess wasn't losing any ground. I had never seen him at Muldowney or at any of the meets, but he was handling his machine like a veteran.

At the end of the natural whoop-de-doo terrain, the course made a 90-degree turn into a long U that would bring us out onto the beach. The first half of it was a continuation of the logging road, the fastest surface on the course since the macadam.

I had enough under me to take the Harleys here. I made no move, waiting for my lesson on the dunes.

Jess was not as patient. He shot past us, past the Harleys, and was halfway through the long U-turn when we reached it. If he was the mech who had modified that bike, Aram had a peer.

The turn was behind us, with straight going ahead, when Jess streaked into the dune area. Even from this distance, I could see he was a believer in the Marty Kaprelian technique.

He hit the first hummock under full gun. The

Oriole soared like a jet plane toward the crest of the second—and buried both wheels to the hubs.

He was still trying to lift it out when we went past on the firmer ground below. The teacher in front confirmed my technique, following the lines I had decided on yesterday. When we came out onto the same strip of macadam that served the starting area, I shifted into top gear and passed both bikes.

At the end of lap one, I was number one, but not misled into a false sense of security. The luck of the draw had granted me the uncluttered and unchallenged early going; traffic was bound to get heavier.

The man on the Marlowe, Hans Nevel, was the first challenger for my temporary crown. He came jolting along the rough ground of the curve before the first jump, bringing back memories of Oasis City.

It could have been coincidence, it could have been a part of his psychic strategy. If his memory was sound, he must have remembered that *he* had been the one who had spilled.

This jump was wide enough for both of us, but the quickest and safest route into it and over it was on the left. On the approach between the trees, I stayed far enough on the left to leave him no passing room on that side.

He made his move on my right well before the

takeoff. The way I read him, he must have thought he had enough torque to get past and cut in front of me before we were airborne.

The Oriole took it personally, snarling as I twisted it higher, digging for the incline, scattering pine needles at the Marlowe.

Up and over, flying free and alone, landing well, heading into the S curve before the hairpin, the whine of the Marlowe growing dimmer every second.

I didn't look back until we reached the straight stretch after the hairpin. Not a bike was in sight! That should have been comforting. I found it puzzling. Unless there had been a mass crackup behind us, there should have been at least half a dozen bikes in sight in a field of this caliber.

There had been some kind of trouble, probably minor, I learned, as I rode unchallenged toward the starting line. Ahead, the yellow caution flag was waving.

Slow down, that meant, *and maintain position.*

The order to maintain position couldn't hurt me. The order to slow down could. A second-place rider, a half-lap behind, could slow down just enough to pull up two feet behind me and still be maintaining his position.

If the trouble was serious, the caution flag would not be waving. The race would have been halted.

Two miles later, at the uphill jump, I saw what had happened. The Maico track-blocker from Monterey had crashed on the far side and saturated the landing area with gas and oil. He was helping an official scatter wet sand over it.

There was dry, safe ground to the left of them. Another official signaled me to land on that area. Over I went.

The way I saw it, a third official in the area was warranted. Or the one who had pointed out my jump area could also have flashed an all-clear signal. Because technically I was still riding under the caution warning. There was no way I could be sure that oily jump was the only reason for the warning.

Hans Nevel was sure. Or maybe he didn't care. He came up from behind again, half a mile later, which was legal enough. He zoomed past me on the second curve of the S, which was illegal.

He was really streaking. He was out of sight before I came back to the macadam, before I could see the all-clear flag waving in the starter's hand far ahead.

I had been out-foxed.

Don't do anything foolish now, hothead, I warned myself. *Don't blow your cool. You've still got the bike to make it up, if you don't do anything stupid.*

I stilled the resentment bubbling in me. This was not a war, it was a race. I settled for something in between, a mission. Nevel became my goal.

If I stayed up and running, I had the horse to complete the mission. When Paul Wragge pulled alongside on the straight stretch beyond the hairpin, the pace I maintained was designed to catch Hans, not outrun Paul.

His goal was immediate and personal—to get past. When we came to the right-angle turn before the long U, his pace was too personal—and too fast for the angle. His Suzuki went sliding into the grassy bank that framed the turn.

I lost track of laps, searching for the Marlowe ahead in the tailenders I was starting to go by, searching and not finding it. If Hans had gone down, I would have seen him. He had to be up there somewhere.

When Marty made his challenge in the dunes, he, too, must have thought of it as personal. He deserted the showboating he had called fun and took the firmer routes.

Again, our goals were different. He was concerned with getting past. I was determined to keep moving. He found a faster route around one of the dunes and came up onto the macadam ten feet in front of me.

On that straight stretch run over a hard surface, ten feet was a meaningless edge to hold over the

Oriole. I was back to second place two hundred yards later.

I was in the ninth lap before I finally saw a Marlowe ahead. It was shrouded by a trio of lappers. They were impeding his progress.

Easy now, Colin, he's not moving that fast. Don't blow it now. Stay vertical!

I got within striking distance before the start of the U, took the sharp turn as carefully as a school bus driver, moved closer—and learned the rider on the Marlowe was not Nevel.

I moved past the four of them before the last-lap flag waved. The track ahead was clear, no also-rans, no Hans.

Should I go all out? Should I put the needle deep into the red? What was wrong with second place? It was two places higher than my standard finish.

Was it time to dream the impossible dream? I measured it against the fact and settled for the fact. Just a touch faster than the pace I had maintained through the other nine laps, that was the decision I made.

It was clear going; the lappers had all been lapped. They were my allies behind, fighting off the would-be challengers, as I made my solo flight to the checkered flag.

Aram, I thought, was too excited when I pulled in.

"You know what you did?" he asked. "You set a new ten-lap course record!"

"How could I? What about Nevel?"

"Nevel?" He looked blank. "He was waved off the course and disqualified for advancing under the caution flag. Didn't you know that?"

I shook my head.

"The jerk!" he said. "I really told him off."

"You shouldn't have," I said. "He won me a race."

11

Brad had taken over my fourth-place slot, Kowalski of Clovis had finished ninth. It had been a great day for Delta. And it had been a great day for the riders from the San Joaquin Valley; Marty Kaprelian had finished third, only half a length behind Don Dunphy.

At Houston, Elkins had led all the way until a piston had cracked in the final lap. Kelly Tanner of Detroit had won more than the race on his Harley; he had moved up to National Number One. They both would be at the Valdesto hundred-miler. That should help attendance.

On Monday, I had an interview visit from a writer for *Coast Cycle Weekly.* On Wednesday, I had a headline in the same paper. It was on one of the inner pages, but it was still a headline.

THREE WINS IN THREE WEEKS, the headline read. And under it, a subhead—*Is Delta Coming Back?*

Brad must have been interviewed, too, because his two wins at Muldowney were reported, along with some quotes. But Seacliff was the big Pacific Division traditional, and the new record got more ink than either of us. All the former record holders were listed.

"I notice you didn't mention me," Aram said.

"I mentioned you a dozen times! Only about a tenth of what I said was printed."

He grinned. "I know. I was eavesdropping Monday. Take a look at the listings."

Seacliff was a high-point meet. I had jumped to sixth place. Brad was eighth, Marty seventh.

"Maybe," Aram said, "the time has come to see about leasing or buying that empty store next door."

"Or maybe," I said, "we had better wait until I meet the big boys again. There weren't many national rankers at Seacliff."

"You set a course record, junior!"

"I know. But did you read the names of the former record holders? If we didn't live out here, we wouldn't have recognized them. Seacliff has always been a top Division race, but it has never awarded National points."

Aram smiled. "I'm getting this feeling you're looking forward to meeting the big boys again."

"I only compete with myself, Aram."

"Unless somebody gets in your way. Why do you always call the National rankers the big boys?"

I didn't answer.

"Big boys are nice, too," he said. "I'm a big boy."

"We've got a lot of work lined up," I said. "Let's get to it."

There would be a couple of names I wouldn't be competing against at Valdesto. Elkins would be running a 250 and Gary Park a big Harley. The Dunphys would be running in our class. Neither had a chance at the overall title; their best hope to climb higher was in the small cycle rankings.

And there would be some hot easterners running the lightweights, including last year's national champion, Kelly Tanner, now eight points ahead of Elkins in this year's overall title chase.

On Thursday, an ancient and noisy Chev panel truck pulled up next to our discount gas pump. "Three gallons," the driver said, grinning, "unless my credit's good here."

It was the kid from Clovis, Jess Kowalski. I said, "Because you did not tarnish the proud name of Delta last week, I am going to put in ten gallons, free."

"Hey, no!" he said.

"Hey, yes," I said. "I suppose you'll be at Valdesto Pines?"

He shook his head. "That's in Oregon, man! Ten

gallons won't take me that far. And neither will this heap."

"Jess," I asked, "did you drive all the way here from Clovis to buy three gallons of gas—or bum a ride to Valdesto?"

"You're embarrassing me," he said.

"We'll pick you up," I said. "What's the address?"

"I'll meet you here. What time?"

"Two o'clock Saturday afternoon. Bring your own grub."

After he left, I phoned Dykstra in San Jose and told him I needed a couple more tires for that Valdesto surface. "There's a hot local privateer who's running a Delta there," I explained. "The same kid who took ninth at Seacliff."

"If you mean Jess Kowalski," Dykstra said, "we've already shipped them to him. He phoned here yesterday, asking if we sold tires at a discount. He casually mentioned his success at Seacliff, so we sent him some tires—free."

"He told me five minutes ago he hadn't planned on making Valdesto!"

"He said something about not getting transportation. Didn't you say he was going to be there?"

"I did. We're taking him. He's really cute, that kid."

Dykstra laughed. "That's what this firm needs on

the firing line, enterprising young men. Good luck to all of you."

Hustler would be a more accurate description, I thought, a thought I voiced to Aram.

He shook his head. "Enterprising is the right word. Remember, we've never been hungry. We can't judge others from our background."

"He poor-mouthed me out of ten gallons of gas, too."

"Why, that little hustler!" Aram said.

Jess looked sheepish, I thought, when he loaded his extra tires on the truck.

"Did you bring your food?" I asked him.

He grinned. "Of course! You think I'm a freeloader?"

"Aram and I haven't voted on you yet. Dykstra thinks you're an enterprising young man."

"Sarge, when you're as poor as I am and as small as I am, you have to be pushy, if you want to survive. I won't crowd you; I'll ride in the box."

"No, you won't. You'll ride in front. There's plenty of room in the cab for two small, pushy guys and Aram."

He had come to Clovis two years ago, from Milwaukee, he told us. He had come to live with an aunt there, but it hadn't panned out. He worked in a hamburger stand at night and part time in a filling station during the day, and lived in a furnished room.

"Are your folks still in Milwaukee?" I asked him.

"My father's dead," he said. "My mother married again. I didn't get along with—with him. My aunt in Clovis is my father's sister. But she—well, she isn't anything like he was, so I moved out."

"How old were you when you left Milwaukee?"

He smiled. "If I told you that, you'd know how old I am now. And I could lose my AMA card."

"I'm not an informer, Jess."

"I was fourteen when I came to Clovis," he said. "I'd been racing the Wisconsin tracks since I was twelve." He took a breath. "I was big for my age, until I got to be twelve."

Aram said, "Your father let you race when you were twelve years old?"

"Sure. We both raced, every summer, mostly on those county-fair tracks. That was one great time in my life."

Nothing from me. Nothing from Aram.

"So that," Jess said quietly, "is why I wanted to buy your old Oriole. Deltas were the only bikes Pop and I ever rode."

The kid was already into us for ten gallons of gas and a free ride. But after a story like that, when he broke out what he called his dinner, two peanut-butter sandwiches on supermarket bread, could we let him sit there and smell those fat hamburgers cooking and not offer him one?

"You guys are sure great," he said. "It's going to hurt, beating you tomorrow, Sarge."

"This is a one-mile, hard-surface track," I reminded him, "not a county-fair bull ring. And Aram tuned my bike."

"I know. The track at the state fairgrounds in Milwaukee is a paved mile, too. And I rode it often. I figured Aram would give my bike a once-over in the morning. I mean, we're all Delta riders, right?"

I looked at Aram and Aram laughed. He said, "Hustler, I'll tell you what I'll do. I'll tune your bike every meet we're together, if you promise to write to your mother every week."

"Why should I write to her, married to that jerk?"

"Never mind the 'why.' Is it a deal, or not?"

"Okay, I promise."

"And if I find out you broke your promise," Aram said, "I'll break your arm."

"I never broke a promise in my life," Jess said.

Hustler, he might be, but I believed him. He was the purse-size Melvin T. Muldowney.

There was very little on Jess' bike that needed improving, Jess discovered next morning.

"Are you sure?" Jess asked. "Remember, even though we're competitors, we're still brothers in Delta."

"One more remark like that out of you, skinny, and this bike will be your transportation home."

"I'm sorry. It was a dumb thing to say. C'mon, Sarge, let's try out the track."

"You take it easy out there," Aram said. "That is one fast slick track. I'm talking to both of you."

Papa Aram had adopted another son. We both nodded.

Slick was the wrong word for the track; the traction was fine. What made it dangerous was its flatness. There was no bank to it that I could notice. A rider could build up tremendous speeds on these long straightaways—and overcharge the flat corners.

It looked to me as if someone had taken a pair of adjoining airplane runways and connected them with turns. I learned later that was the story; it was an abandoned airport.

We loafed along, getting the feel of it, testing how far over we could lean through the bends. Brad went past us when we were loafing, and went past us again before we finished our seven-lap cruise.

"It's not anything like that Milwaukee mile," Jess said. "These corners make me nervous."

Brad went past the pits, still steaming. "He's really hungry, isn't he?" Jess said.

"Brad? No. His folks are well off."

"That isn't what I meant. The boys have told me

the story of you two. You started competing in the cradle. And now you've got three wins in a row."

"Brad and I are friends, Jess."

He smiled. "You and I are friends, too. But I'm still hungry."

I wanted to say, *I only compete with myself,* but I had said it too often. So I said, "Let's go out and heckle Brad."

We came up behind him on the third round, went past him in the backstretch, Jess on the right, me on the left. I could hear him revving up behind as I leaned through the turn. He was not about to let us go unchallenged.

We were braking into the pits, and laughing, when he stormed past.

"Funny fellows!" he said, when he came in, a lap later.

"We were testing your reaction time, Brad," I told him. "Do you know Jess Kowalski?"

"Yup. How do you guys like these turns?"

"We don't," Jess said. "But we can lean into them deeper than the big cycles."

"We're not competing against the big machines, Jess," I reminded him.

He grinned. "Speak for yourself. I compete with everything that's out there."

Jess Kowalski versus the world. It was a big world, but Goliath had been a big man—until he tangled with David. Don't take the kid lightly, world, don't make Goliath's mistake.

The Goliaths were running the track now, Kelly Tanner on a light Harley, Gary Park on its big brother, Army on a 250 Husky. They didn't challenge each other, saving it for the afternoon when it would pay off.

Sunday money or Sunday fun? Was it still fun for them? It had to be. No sane man would stick with a trade as noisy, smelly, dangerous, and poorly paid as this unless he enjoyed it.

That Sunday at Valdesto Pines, I must report, was not one of my brighter afternoons. What kept it from being a total washout was the Delta. As Aram had guessed, there wasn't another 125 in the field that topped out higher. Head to head, down those long straightaways, I outran every 125 I dueled with.

But those unbanked turns. . . . There were no upper fences guarding them; they were edged with bales of straw, a lucky break for me. Bales of straw are softer than six-by-six posts or two-by-eight fencing. I bounced into them three times in the first twenty-five laps but went down only once.

The bounces didn't lose me any ground. The spill dropped me from third place to ninth. What was more defeating, it taught me to have too much respect for those flat turns. In the next fifteen miles, I advanced only one place.

Riding eighth was an insult to the Oriole. But staying vertical, I almost convinced myself, was the smartest way to keep in contention. There were a lot of riders bouncing into those bales.

At the halfway point, this sensible decision had lost me no ground. Nor had it gained me any. There was an "8" on Aram's board, and a big question mark below it.

If safe-and-sane Aram wondered at the slowness of our pace, we were loafing. I twisted a few more revs out of the Oriole and came up behind the Stockton whiz, Paul Wragge, early in the backstretch.

I hadn't passed him in the first fifty miles, and he had started ahead of me. Unless he had made a visit to the pits, he had to be higher on the ladder.

I dogged him closely through the stretch, letting him know I was there. I lost ground through the turn, due to my overcaution. I came out twenty yards behind the Suzuki, with the long straight track ahead.

It was time to try a new technique. It might burn out the brakes, eventually, but maybe the Delta's superior speed could make up for my inferior courage in the turns.

I charged past the Suzuki in the first hundred yards and was going full out by the time I passed the pits. A few seconds short of the corner, I jammed both binders and downshifted.

The warning smell of smoke drifted up from the tires and the brakes. I would need to adjust this technique to something less drastic, or they could burn out before I reached the checkered flag.

It worked in that lap. I had advanced to seventh place, according to the board. *Careful now; this could be a disaster road.* The tires should hold up. The brakes would be my problem.

I was not the only rider following the pattern. In the sixty-third lap, I was keeping pace with Kelly Tanner in the backstretch, trailing him closely when he braked for the turn—too late.

He bounced into the first bale and off it, still in control. It was the second bale that sent him spinning, and me into sixth place.

Advancing only one place in twelve laps meant the leaders were running this track faster than I was. I hadn't noticed any brake fade so far. I decided to take a chance on running the corners deeper before slowing.

Again, it worked. Don Dunphy and Marty were running neck and neck along the grandstand straightaway, both of them gaining on Don's brother, a hundred feet in front of them.

Dan was using the delayed brake technique. Don and Marty were not. I slid past them before the turn and was crowding Dan halfway through it.

I went past him early in the rear stretch and almost lost my lead in the second turn. He was really charging those corners.

I picked up the lost yards in the front straight. The board informed me I was finally back to where I had been before the spill—in third place.

Dan Dunphy didn't want me there, and he was making it personal. Lap after lap, he kept crowding me through the corners, trying to force me wide, so he could get past below.

We must have been putting on the best show in the ring; the crowd noise drowned out the whine of our engines every time we went past the stands. Evidently the heavyweights, who had to be well in front, were putting on a dull act. But what about our lightweight peers? There were two of them somewhere ahead of us.

The pace Dunphy had forced on me should have them in sight. I knew the current national leader, Kelly Tanner, wasn't one of them. I had passed him thirty laps back and hadn't seen him since. I knew which bikes had led through the laps before my spill. But so many of them had been in and out of the pits since, I couldn't be sure which two were still in front.

Ninety-three miles of piercing engine whine and nerve-stretching competition on a tight-cornered track had taken its toll. I was tired and aching and tense. Dunphy's pressure had brought me to the rim of my ability on this course. I should have realized that.

My brain must have been as tired as my body; I stepped up the pace. The Oriole had covered as many miles as I had and was just as subject to wear and tear.

The brakes were still working, but not well enough to handle the speed with which I hit the next turn. For the second time in the race, I went down, sliding into the bales at the apex of the turn.

The engine didn't die. I was up again and running in a matter of seconds—enough seconds to drop me from third place to sixth, where I finished.

12

"Tough luck," Aram said.

I shrugged.

"That was some show you and Dan put on. You had 'em standing on their seats, man!"

"I should have stayed with that act. Where did Dan finish?"

"Third." He grinned. "Guess who won."

"I'm too tired for guessing games, Aram."

"The kid from Clovis," he said. "Go over and congratulate him."

Jess was sitting sideways on the seat of the pickup, the door open. He was taking the boot off his left foot. "I twisted an ankle," he explained. "That is one dumb track, right?"

"Not for you. Congratulations."

"Thank you. But any time I finish ahead of Kelly Tanner, you can bet there's something wrong with the track."

"Where did he finish?"

"About an inch behind me. He went past you when you were down and kept moving up. Through the last five laps, he was camping in my hair."

Goliath had met David. I asked, "Why this sudden attack of modesty?"

He smiled. "I still need a ride home. It's been a great day for Delta. Brad finished ninth."

And a better day for Jess Kowalski, I thought. *Don't be a sore loser, Colin.* I said, "I'll admit it's a dumb track if you'll agree it takes an all-around expert to win on it."

"Okay. Will you get me some ice from the chest to wrap around this ankle?"

We did better than that. We put the ice chest on the floor of the cab and he rode home with his foot in it. That didn't give me much floor room for my own feet, but my heart was full of compassion for this defenseless little victim of a broken home. Oh, yes. . . .

We loaded his bike in the ancient panel truck for him at the station and wrapped his ankle. And Aram told him, "You write to your ma now, *this week!* Maybe you'd better send the letter to me so I know it will be mailed."

"No need, Aram," Jess said quietly. "I'm going to send her some money, too. I made enough today."

The old Chev rattled off, and Aram watched its

taillights vanish down the street. "Some kid," he said. "One real gutsy kid."

"Who could put us out of business," I said.

"Sarge," he said sternly, "you conned me into this nonsense with that Sunday-fun line of yours. If it's not fun any more, let's give it up."

"Not me," I said. "I'm one real gutsy kid."

Monday made Sunday look like a picnic. Our wealthiest customer had bought a set of premium radials for his Cadillac a month back, and now the manufacturer had decided to recall them because of some dangerous defects.

I tried to explain to this irate knothead that Aram and I had not manufactured the tires, and if we had, there would be no reason we would want him involved in an accident, which he more or less implied.

I was about five seconds short of punching him in his big paunch when Aram came out and took over the discussion.

An hour later, I was trying to loosen a head nut on a well-rusted engine when the wrench broke. I watched the blood seep up through the black grease on my knuckles and *almost* threw the wrench through the front window.

It rattled off the wall below the window and bounced over to where Aram was working.

He looked at the wrench and then at me. "Why

don't you wash up," he suggested, "and deliver Doc Williams' car? There's no hurry on that job. The owner's on vacation."

"Lee can deliver Doc's car when he comes," I said. "I'll wash my hand and get us a couple of Cokes. I'm sorry, Aram."

"Sure." He smiled. "I'll bet that sixth place yesterday will move you up in the rankings."

"That isn't why I blew my stack. I wasn't even thinking about racing!"

"If you say so, partner. But it would be the first day in ten years that you weren't. Be sure to clean that hand well, and put some peroxide on those knuckles."

Tuesday was quieter. Wednesday brought the *Coast Cycle Weekly.* I had advanced to fourth place, Brad to seventh. The Elkins-Tanner contest was still close. Army had won the 250 at Valdesto and was now only three points below Tanner nationally.

The days were getting shorter and the nights cooler. The competition at Muldowney Raceway stayed hot.

M.T. had originally advertised it as the Ascot of Northern California. It was now outdrawing Ascot in attendance and topping it in purses. Considering the difference in climate and population, and the fact that M.T. had never instituted night racing, he had achieved a remarkable feat of promotion.

He had also made it tougher for us loyal locals. We loyal locals had responded by buying better machines. The local dealers had responded by sending their mechanics as pit crews and giving generous discounts on parts to the riders of their machines.

All of which combined, of course, to make Melvin T. Muldowney richer. I was beginning to believe he deserved to be.

Brad and Marty joined me in the Pacific Top Five on the same Sunday, a forty-mile motocross at Mill Junction. Brad took a second, Marty a fifth, your humble narrator a fourth. Jess Kowalski, now known as the Clovis Comet, won it. But Jess had started too late in the season to hope for a high-point ranking —this year.

Very few of the national rankers had been at Mill Junction. They would not have made much difference. It had been a national meet for decades, until last year. Jess' time shattered the old record and earned him a write-up in *Cycle World.*

First Marty and now Jess; the newcomers were getting the ink. It was a young man's game, and I would be a senile nineteen in November. That's a joke.

On an overcast Sunday, at the "Muldowney Raceway of the south" called Ascot, I picked up both Pacific and National points in the J. C. Agajanian super-deluxe, star-studded (his adjectives), twenty-lap feature. J.C. was the original cowboy-hat race promoter. To him, Melvin T. was just an *odar* newcomer.

What was more important to me than making second in the Division rankings (and thirty-second in the National) was beating the Clovis Comet.

I had developed a thing about Jess, a childish and shameful resentment at his being so good so early. The track was alien to both of us, but I came from half a lap back in the sixteenth lap to nip him by a few feet at the flag for second place.

Elkins had won, Tanner had finished fourth. They now shared the National top spot.

"You were terrific," Jess told me on the ride home. "If you had made your move earlier, you would have creamed Elkins."

"Beating you is enough for one day."

"Sarge, we're buddies!"

"*Now,* we're buddies. I hate to admit it, but I was beginning to resent you. That's creepy, isn't it?"

Jess chuckled. "I forgive you. I wasn't too crazy about you, either, when you edged me at the wire today. What we must remember is that there is always next week."

"What both of you should remember," Aram said, "is that racing is a sport. And if you're not sportsmen, you shouldn't be in it."

Jess nudged me, and we said it together: "Yes, papa."

We would be back at Ascot for the 125 finale of the season in two weeks. Next week, we would travel to the desert run at Dune.

Dune was a Division meet. The riders still trying to climb the National ladder would be at St. Louis. The western privateers who were out of that point race probably would come to Dune. The pay was better.

Sixty-four miles of desert survival test, that was Dune. There would be thirty-two miles due east, through sand, past rocks, between the chaparral, and along dry stream beds, to Cactus Flats. The check point was there, and the turnaround point. Then we would head back to Dune, squinting into the afternoon sun.

It had been fun, when I was young and dumb. I didn't enjoy it this time. A hundred and twelve noisy bikes churning up dust and sand over the bleak, littered desert—not a pleasant way to spend a Sunday.

The amateurs were there in great numbers, the rank and the ranking, the bathed and the unbathed. It was the kind of meet that furnishes ammunition for the enemies of motorcyling.

Jess didn't go with us. As he explained it, he was not riding a bike he didn't own, as I was. And he thought too much of his Oriole to risk it against some of the wild cycle-gang refugees on their road hawgs that the Dune run attracted.

Call it a mixed Sunday. It wasn't fun, but it was profitable. The bearded fatsos on their road hawgs met an adversary not impressed by their bulk or their belligerence, the American desert. The professionals and the washed amateurs gave it the respect it demanded, and prevailed.

Among the 125-cc professionals in the field, Colin Sergenian finished second, about four lengths behind that expert guitar player and AMA novice, Marty Kaprelian. Marty's win earned him second place in the Division. My finish put me into a precarious first place, five points in front of Marty. Brad and Don Dunphy were still in the running for the title. That would be decided at Ascot.

Army Elkins, last year's champ, was out of the Division race; he had missed too many of our meets. But he and Tanner would probably fight it out for the National all-class title, depending on how they had finished at St. Louis. That, too, could be decided at Ascot.

"First place," Aram said on the ride home. "I suppose that makes this miserable meet worthwhile."

"Barely. I sure never expected, in May, to climb this high. It's crazy, isn't it?"

"I figure it ten-ten-eighty," he said.

"Come again?"

"Ten percent for your skill, ten percent for my wrench—but the eighty percent has to go to Delta. Maybe those foreign bikes won't be flooding the market, if Delta stays in business."

"They'll stay in business. Over the long haul, quality always wins."

He smiled. "We'll see, at Ascot, next Sunday."

We would see nothing at Ascot next Sunday. On Tuesday, the fringe of a tropical storm hit the Los Angeles area, setting a new 24-hour rainfall record, a record that was broken on Wednesday. It tapered off after that, but the county was already afloat. Ascot was under water.

The Agajanian of the north, Melvin Terence Muldowney, rode to the rescue of the AMA. He had the track and the stands worthy of an AMA season finale, and they knew it. As a benevolent gesture, he promised he would not even raise his ticket or refreshment prices. As a business gesture, he announced that his Armenian dress-alike, Ascot's J. C. Agajanian, would be his guest of honor. M.T. did not make enmities he could profitably avoid.

So we had two white cowboy hats bobbing through the pits, two genial extroverts wishing one and all the best of luck.

At St. Louis the week before, Elkins had gone out

with a burned clutch, Tanner with a jammed transmission. They were still sharing the top of the heap.

There would be twenty 125-cc cycles, a field limited to the top ten Division riders and the top ten National, or their alternates. We would fight it out through forty laps on this track we had built and M.T. had made famous.

"Tough field," I told Aram. "All the big boys."

"Don't worry about them. You worry about Marty. You finish in the first five, and it's your title. Even if you finish sixth, he'd have to win to tie you."

"That might be interesting," I said, "to an accountant. I am not an accountant."

"I've noticed that. That's why I have always handled our account books. Just remember we're working for Delta."

"No," I said. *"With* them, not *for* them. We work for us, partner."

He sighed. He started to say something, decided not to, and went over to yak with Joe Gehrig in the next pit.

From the pit on the other side, Jess said, "You shouldn't argue with Aram. He's usually right."

"But not always. Would you settle for fifth right now?"

"Sarge, why ask the question when you know the answer? Luck, buddy."

"And to you. It should be a great race."

"Only if I win it," he said.

Brad came over to tell me, "I've still got a chance, you know. Don't look so smug."

"That's my false front. Do you realize, if you weren't a gentleman, you might be top man on the totem pole now?"

"How do you mean?"

"I picked up ten points that afternoon you missed because of your sister's wedding."

"I remember. There's always next year." He paused. "And there's still this year. Luck, champ."

"To all of us," I said. "Brothers in Delta."

"Yuck!" Brad said, and "Ugh!" Jess said, and then it was time to go out and line up.

There were two rows, ten bikes to each row, under the eagle eye of Doc Kucera, who had supervised the lottery. He didn't have the green flag. Honored guest J. C. Agajanian would flash the starting signal—when Doc told him to.

Paul Wragge and Don Dunphy, the best of the anticipaters, moved out quickly at the jumpoff from their first-row slots. They led the field into the first turn. From the second-row pole, the Oriole and I stayed close to the inner rail. These were not amateurs, jamming the lower track. Each rider sought his own groove.

There was some daylight in the track ahead; I moved past four of the front liners and led all of the second-row bikes into the turn. That put us into seventh place.

From eleventh to seventh in less than 220 yards is a fair advance. I settled for that around the turn and into the rear straight.

Ahead of us, the leading six were bunched, fighting for the first-lap advantage. With thirty-nine-and-a-half laps to go, I made no move to join them. The quickest way to go down is to get involved in fast and heavy traffic. They would string out eventually.

My serious problems were still behind. Army was back there, and Marty and Tanner and Jess and Brad.

Though the day was cool for the San Joaquin Valley, it was warm enough to overheat high-revving, air-cooled engines through forty laps of dusty competition. *Patience, Colin.*

The high-pointers behind must have been thinking along the same line. In the next four laps, not one came up to challenge. Two of the front-runners had tangled on the near turn and gone down. I rode fifth.

The first to come up, of course, was the Clovis Comet. He passed me in the backstretch and leaned deeply into the turn at a speed I wasn't ready for. His dragging left foot threw up a geyser of dust as he tempted the law of gravity. At that speed, he could wind up with a broken ankle when the track got rougher.

Go, Jess, go. Enjoy your early moment of glory. The big test was far ahead. I rode sixth.

Aram agreed with this philosophy. There was one word on the board: "Smart!" When you agree with Aram, you're smart—in his view. In his dictionary, that means sensible.

Brad was the next to come up, but he didn't challenge. Maybe he thought my sense of pace was better than his, maybe he hoped to trigger me into deserting it. Whatever, he haunted me for three laps before dropping back.

I was one-quarter of the way to the flag and still riding sixth. Fifth was high enough to preserve my crown. Fifth was high enough for Marty to take it away, if I didn't finish. His Yamaha came alongside in the middle of the rear straightaway.

I had the inner groove and the faster bike. He had his dream. For six laps, we fought it out, while Aram waved the board to get my attention. I knew what it read: "E-Z!"

This is not an easy trade, Aram; the competition is too mean. In the seventeenth lap, sanity prevailed and the dream moved past. I was back to seventh.

In the nineteenth lap, I was again sixth, as Marty's Yamaha went smoking into his pit.

The crown was now firmer on my head. Brad and

171

Don were still in the running, and Don was somewhere in front of us. But it would take more number sense than I had to figure out the mathematics involved.

One thing I was sure of: they would need their best effort of the season to top my point count—if I stayed vertical.

In the twenty-eighth lap, Aram's board had a big "5" on it. Four pits beyond his sign, I saw the reason. Don's bike had joined Marty's in the Yamaha pit.

Okay, Brad, make your move. You are the last pretender to the throne. He didn't. Tanner went by and so did Army, with only a token resistance from me. I was back to seventh in the thirty-second lap.

Some other front-runner must have gone to the pits in that lap. There was a "6" on the board and no downed bikes in sight. From here in, it should be a milk run.

It could have been. Maybe it should have been. Maybe I was bored, maybe I am just dumb. But in the thirty-seventh lap, riding fourth, the trio in front finally came into view.

The Clovis Comet, Tanner, and Elkins were streaking past the pits as I slid out of the near turn.

Jess led them into the far turn, but not out of it. Gravity had decided enough was enough. His Oriole went down, sliding up the bank, as Kelly and Army moved past below.

That could have been the trigger. Brad still behind and Jess down; who would defend the honor of Delta? Aram was a sensible man, but his unpublished uncle must be given his due. What a sorry thing a fact is, measured against a dream.

There was time, and I had the horse. *Why not?* I thought. *Why not?* the Oriole whined. A twist of the wrist was all that was needed.

They had their private battle. They probably didn't even know I was moving up through the next two laps. The Oriole's tach was beyond the red, but no higher than my faith in my machine.

It looked most hopeless in the backstretch of the final lap. They were all out, the National crown in sight. There was no way I could trust my present skill to keep me vertical through the turn at that speed.

They had the skill to do it, and they did it, though they missed the upper rail by inches. But there are times, as I have mentioned before, when the shorter route is faster than the faster route. I had the shorter route. We came out of the turn three abreast.

Do I have to tell you the rest? I was the only rider on a Delta Oriole and the track was clear and straight ahead. Army was second, Kelly third.

Army was the new National Champion, but we had met again and I had beat him to the flag.

"You're absolutely crazy!" Aram told me in the pit.

"That's why he's out there," Jess said. "You deserve to be Number One, Sarge." He paused, and smiled. "Until next year."

"Until next year," I agreed.

About the Author

WILLIAM CAMPBELL GAULT loved to write poems in high school but he submitted them to the school paper under a fictitious name, as the fellows he hung around with looked dimly at peers with poetic inclinations. He ended his formal education during his freshman year at the University of Wisconsin one cold day when the temperature reached nineteen degrees below zero. Four freshmen climbed into his little Essex roadster—as driver he did not have to draw straws to see who got the rumble seat—and took off for Miami.

The depression was under way but Mr. Gault finally found a job in a shoe factory, in Wisconsin, working days and writing nights, and finally sold his first short story in 1936. Becoming a full-time writer in 1941, he was called up and served for three years in the army.

Leaving his hometown of Wauwatosa, Wisconsin, (a suburb of Milwaukee) after forty years, William Gault made the move to California where he now resides in Santa Barbara. He has written three hundred short stories, thiry-five young adult sports novels, and twenty-two adult mystery novels.

When the author uses an Armenian background in his books, he does so with authenticity. His sister married an Armenian, so he became a double brother-in-law when he married the sister of his sister's husband. They have one son, one daughter, and four grandchildren.